Vineyards
of
Love

Vineyards

of

Love

Pooja Srivastava

Woven Words Publishers OPC Pvt. Ltd.

Registered Office:

Vill: Raipur, P.O: Raipur Paschimbar,

Dist: Purba Midnapore, Pin: 721401,

West Bengal, India.

www.wovenwordspublishers.in

Email: editor@wovenwordspublishers.in

First published by Woven Words Publishers OPC Pvt. Ltd., 2017

Copyright© Pooja Srivastava, 2017

NOVELLA

IMPRINT: WOVEN WORDS LAUNCHPAD

ISBN 13: 978-93-86897-12-1

ISBN 10: 9386897121

Price: $8/₹150

Printed and bound in India

PROLOGUE:

I heard footsteps as if someone was following me, while I was returning from a late-night party with friends. I didn't have enough courage to turn around and see who it was, as it was really late and apart from a few stray dogs there was no sign of human presence around. After walking for a while, I couldn't fathom the curiosity and I turned around to see who it was. All I could figure out, in the darkness were two eyes silently staring at me.

I was terrified by the silence of the night and looked at those eyes trying to look for a sign of movement. There was an inexplicable power clouding my judgments. Those eyes glinted and a scent passed through all the remoteness. I stood there, fascinated, captivated and turned back to bow and elope with huge steps. Those eyes chased me with concentration. Their gravity compelled me to stop and surrender myself. The gravity of those eyes showed that I was the only person alive.

The moon shone outside the layer of darkness and my heart stopped beating. The shallow layer of darkness was lit in a glaze. I could now begin to see who it was as the shadow's strong feet tediously overtook my speed and continued to walk towards me. I wanted it to turn back and go. All this while my heart pounded against my ribs with thuds. As the figure moved past darkness and turned towards me, I could clearly see the face of a man illuminated by the street lights. He was someone I didn't want to see, Gautam.

He looked at me through his mesmerising black eyes. His extreme stare shook me inside out and I looked for some narrow alley to flee. There was a dark tunnel at a distance of fifty metres from him. Few gamblers were sitting at the entrance covering the circle around a bonfire, playing cards. Perhaps I could see them because of the fire, but they could not see us. I ran with a bolt to escape from here. As I tried to run past him, he stood in front of me blocking my way. It seemed he was proving my weakness to leave that place without his permission. Each time I tried to escape, his hands stopped me. He held my hands when I tried freeing myself and with every attempt, his grip tightened, and my blue bracelet broke into shards cutting his palm.

He stared sturdily at me with his eyes more determined than ever. He left my hand and pulled me closer. I shut my eyes in anticipation and hit him on his stomach in an attempt to break loose but all my efforts went in vain. I wept, shouted and asked him to leave me. He put his hands on my mouth to subdue my yelling and embraced me tightly, denying any chance to escape. He had been following me for days and wasn't going to leave me easily. His face smelled of strong aftershave. I stared back at his eyes with tears in mine. I made one last attempt to get out of his grip but he wouldn't let me go. I gave up and hid my face in his shirt.

'Let me go please' I wept and said. He kept looking at me with tears in his eyes. 'I love you,' he said in a low mumble.

I silently rested my head on his heart and let my tears blot on his shirt while he heard my sobs. He wiped my tears, held a drop in his palm to stop it from falling on the ground and looked at it as if he had found a tender butterfly enlightening his skin from the air.

'I love you' he said one more time. I raised my head gently to look at his face and soon resumed my earlier position. I didn't know what to say. I knew he loved me. He knew I loved him.

I wanted to run away from him, but secretly I wanted to hold on to him till I couldn't breathe. He completed me in a way I never imagined anyone could ever. There was a sense of reconciliation in his voice that made me even more addicted to him. His breath, smell, eyes and whenever he held my hands, it made me lose all my sanity. I surrendered myself completely to him. I couldn't bear his absence. He made me go crazy; crazy for him. It was just like romantic stories or movies where a couple in a relationship always wanted more of themselves every time. He protected me, from the sinful eyes of the world, holding my insecurities, granting me love, gifting me madness, until I reached the end of my obsession.

'Please leave me,' I said with my face still hidden in his shirt.

My voice was in symphony with his heart. He gleamed with an aura being reflected in the light. I put my hands on his face; His face was moist with tears. My heart hurt, I held my emotions and tried to control the pain. He put his hand on my chest and mine already on his and a pulse moved between us.

Gautam lowered his face shadowing mine and for a moment I forgot everything. I closed his bloodshot eyes with my hands. His swollen eyes said everything that I never wanted to accept. His face came near mine and I felt his warm breath. I stood there denying any possibility of coming closer. He opened his teary eyes and I shut mine in anticipation. He pushed me away with a jerk and moved two steps back. I was not scared of him, but of my own convictions.

The night grew denser and vaguely put a boundary between us blurring his face. The moon floated higher. Night predators made noise in the jungle by the side of alley. Gautam and I stood slit apart by the gap that existed only for the sake of it. There was weariness in his grip now, as he felt weighed down. He turned and walked away. I stared at him, until he was lost in the dense pelt of fog.

GAUTAM

Gautam was a photographer by profession. I used to sneak in his studio just to be around him when he clicked pictures. He smiled and made gestures by his hands instructing a few poses to the models. He had one passion and devotion – Photography. The moment I met him for the first time, I had a strange feeling of comfort around him. He stood there, treading in my mind, strangely taking over all its territory to his possession. He was my senior in office and used to mentor me. I looked blankly at him and never asked anything. My silence was sufficient for him to communicate with.

He loved bringing his younger sister and mother to the studio. His mother was in her fifties, an enigmatic personality. She was a top model in her times but gave up modelling after marriage. She was given the title of 'The glittering glaze' by her husband. Later on, she chose to transfer this title to another model. After quitting modelling, she became the head of the beauty pageant team in her early thirties but later broke ties with the fashion industry. Her judgement was talked of, even now, when she was no longer associated with modelling. The milestone she had set in such a short time was yet to be touched. I often found the models drawing pointers from her. She wore a unique perfume, and it was pretty easy to feel her presence whenever she entered the premises of the studio. Gautam admired her and when she was around, I could clearly see the sense of pride on his face of being her son. It was said that her husband, Mr Amish Sharma, was a jealous person who could not handle her success and was the sole reason behind destroying her career. Theirs was a love marriage. Mr Amish was a drug addict who abandoned his wife and kids to marry an Australian model. Mrs Sharma was in rehab for two years before she could finally overcome her depression. The failure of his parent's marriage had a strong impact on Gautam. He decided that he would never marry. It seemed that he was afraid of, what if; someday he turned out to be like his father. Despite his painful childhood, Gautam possessed a jovial disposition and his manners were refined. We had the least conversation that two people working together could suffice with, but still his voice acted as an encouragement to me. I had to see him at least once in the office to keep my day going.

He was dark and had grave black eyes. Something about him didn't allow me to look into his eyes directly. It always appeared as if the eyes were saying one thing, while lips uttered something else.

We were employed at The Al Da Beatz magazine, where I met him three years ago and since the hour of our acquaintance, he took me by surprise somehow. What I loved most about him, was his originality and the fact that he was so passionate about everything he did. He always said that it was better to learn the hard way; Easier choices never stay long enough with you. When he worked, he worked with passion. When he hated, he hated with passion. When he loved, he loved with passion. His passion made me passionate about him.

Once we went to Mysore on a consignment for the winter collection; after wrapping up, there was a little delay in the arrival of the car. I stood under the shade of a tree, meanwhile he got us coffee. I am anaemic and shivered with cold even in summers, and it was freezing there. He took off his jacket and offered it to me. I asked him to take it back, but he remained silent. Gautam's hands extended towards me, with the jacket as long as I didn't take it. He was in a brown vest and his hands and abs were neatly worked out. The camera was swinging insecurely on his shoulders as he had decided to take a few shots of the street. Nothing could stop me from luring at him while he looked remotely, patiently waiting for the cab and clicked pictures. He was around five feet ten inches tall; there was something about him that made him irresistible. The way he guarded his crew and his family, drew me closer to him.

While we were killing time waiting for the cab, it started drizzling. I hated rain but stood there frozen like the snow-man, watching his silhouette in the starless night below the clouds. He didn't turn around. There was a sudden bolt of lightning. I was not a timid one, but was scared of sudden noise. I put my hands on my ears in reflex. That is when I observed him reading looking at me. I got anxious, for his intense stare was something I couldn't withstand. A smile broke from my lips. I expected him to smile back at me but instead with small footsteps he turned and raised the camera to click my expression. I nodded at him not to take any pictures as

I was all ruffled up, but he suggested me to stand still. One after the other he captured me in the lens, I stood there stupefied. At times when my eyes met his', there was an acute stare that I could not handle. I knew he was just looking at his subject but I never felt for someone with such gravity that resisting the urge to be near him took every drop of my resolve. I felt weak in front of him. His gaze gave me a feeling of being weakened, every time he looked at me. But neither did he say anything nor did I dare to.

I could not understand why I felt a tinge of anger whenever he gave extra attention to any other girl. It was part of our profession, but where was my professionalism? Gautam did nothing to relieve me of my agony; he rarely passed me a smile. We often went on consignments together. His magnetic and hoarse voice pulled me towards him whenever he was around. I found it strange that whenever I heard him laugh, I found myself smiling. He had the joviality of a child. So hearty, that sometimes tears came in my eyes when I heard him laugh.

I would always keep a track of him being in the office but never went to talk to him, just the assurance that he was around, was enough for me to go. I always craved to be around him. I tried escaping his eyes, staring at him from the corner of my eyes. When he stood behind me talking to someone else, I put all the efforts to look at him without turning around. His love soothed me; I was head over heels drowned in his love. But I had seen people in love change. There was always the spark when they were not together, but when they are with each other everything changes. I was curious whether Gautam felt the same, for I lacked conviction. Despite that I didn't want to lose him. Just knowing that he was there, somewhere around me gave me strength. It was surreal. In fact, everything I felt about him was strange. I wanted to possess him, without claiming any authority on him. As I streamed through his desk I heard Kuber speaking,

'Gautam, we have to go on a photo shoot for the hunger strike. It's the cover article for the next edition. Did you hear the political leader Brijesh Sharma is on again? I am sick of their propaganda. Sometimes I wonder do they just pretend or they actually don't eat anything? Whatever it is, I can't sit hungry even if I have to choose between food and life.' And he took a bite of the biscuit in his hand.

'I thought we are going to Assam for the regional festival that is scheduled for this month.' Gautam said looking at his laptop screen working on some picture, ignoring Kuber's remark. He was in a light purple T-shirt and grey cargos. His short hair combed backwards and there was slight beard on his face. He took a sip of his coffee.

'Yeah, I know but Patrick called just now. He said that covering the stupid strike is a priority this month. Someone else can go to Assam. But, they prefer you taking the pictures of the strike.' He took another bite of the biscuit. I was looking at him and his hunger streak made me laugh every time. He was slim and possessed a great physique. He didn't even hit the gym. Everyone, including me, was jealous of his metabolism, for he ate far more than anyone.

'Okay, go and tell them I will do it.' After a sigh, he consciously turned towards Kuber, 'But also, tell him if he wants me to cover the strike, I will, only if they let me cover the tribal festival in Assam.'

His hands rested on the chair while I stood looking uneasily at him. I couldn't understand his emphasis on going there because Assam's event wasn't that big. No sooner did that thought flit through my mind, than I remember how I had once told him that it was my dream place and he had promised to recommend my name the next time for the regional festival at Assam.

I was both ecstatic and confused at the same time. Was he was planning to go there for me, or was he falling for me, or had he already fallen for me? I tried to figure out what was it about. While he could choose to cover many other big events, he wanted to come to Assam. This thought made me feel alive, even if, he was not coming because of me, what matters the most was that he'll be around.

Gautam caught me staring at him and returned the stare with the same intensity which seeped in my pores. I walked away with brisk steps. I was unable to walk properly because his eyes were chasing me. I could not turn around to see if I was out of his sight, but dimly prayed for it. I went to the coffee vending machine and served myself a cup of hot coffee. My mind wanted to relax and think that everything was okay. I cupped my face and shook my head in embarrassment, wishing nothing had happened, and he didn't see me stare at him. I inclined my head towards the machine and sighed. Straightening my top, I picked the coffee mug. I could sense someone standing behind me. I told myself that it was a delusion. Though, my hysterical heartbeat had already amplified.

'It's not him, it's not him there' I told myself thousand times, but could not bring myself to turn around. I took a sip of my coffee, my hands shaking and lips cold. I exhaled in the cup letting the hot coffee vapour hit my face. My face turned red with embarrassment submerged in the coffee mist. I turned almost pale as someone walked past me, making me shrill with fear. I gathered some courage and looked with anxiousness, to my dread it was Gautam. He was there to drink water. I didn't know how to react after what happened just then; his odour paralysed me as he walked. I wanted to leave, while my instinct commanded me to stay. I found myself blushing as he was turning towards me. It appeared as if he wanted to ask, why I was staring at him, did I have something to say. Maybe he looked at me just like that, but it's said we perceive other's as we feel about them.

For around twenty seconds he looked at me without speaking anything and I looked at him pretending to sip my coffee.

I felt as if I'm under surveillance for committing some crime. Something from within urged me to leave. How could he stare at me so unapologetically? My trembling hands could barely hold the mug. The coffee spill on the floor, the mug shook so roughly. I stormed out, not caring about what he was going to think of me. My hand, with which I held the coffee mug, knocked the chair kept there. The cup and chair both fell. I had a scratch due to the chair. What was I doing? Was I mad? I covered my face to escape the embarrassment, turning pale. Before I could say something, the damage was done. The floor was covered with coffee and ruins of the mug. I looked at Gautam with frown; he was smiling now. I was left with a mixture of feelings all of a sudden; Rage, consciousness, humiliation, panic.

I left that place, conveying from my expression, 'You caused this mess, now you clear it.' I hurried back to my desk, face red with anger. The tears were unstoppable. 'How could he smile at me so unapologetically and what does he consider himself? If he is handsome, I am gorgeous too. I am not going to run after him. He is so considerate for others but with me he such a douche. He never talks to me properly, let alone smile. Where does his goodwill go when it comes to me? He behaves as if, I'm an untouchable. All that he manages to do for me is to stare, without blinking an eye. I was getting so uneasy, and instead of leaving, he made me more nervous? How can I love such a person?' Deep down I knew all this was not true. I was instead enraged on myself for getting so vulnerable in front of him.

There was a tap on my shoulder at the same time. I looked up to see Gautam. The thoughts went away all at the pale.

'I am sorry if I made you uncomfortable. Take this coffee.' He looked at me the same as before, though with a perplexed expression. I fumbled for words. He looked breathtakingly handsome. I had rarely seen him this close to me. I stared at him, as if I were drunk by the intensity of his eyes; I could smell his odour.

Overwhelmed by emotions, I said 'Thanks'. I took the coffee mug from his hands and kept it on my desk. My hands were trembling; I tried to contain my nervousness. There was a loud thud when I kept the mug on the table. Gautam gave me a strange look, as if questioning my moves. His hands were shaking too and I tried not to look at them. I could easily guess the series of events but it was impossible to give him any idea about it. He opened his mouth to say something and realized he's shivering. Our eyes met to and fro and Gautam left mumbling something to him. As soon as he left, I turned towards the desk and plunged my face in my palms, resting the elbows on the table. My brows loosened and I shook my head, breathing heavily.

'Breathe, breathe, everything will be fine.' these words were iterating in my mind and I realized I was blushing. Someone tapped on my shoulder again, I turned around and to my surprise it was Gautam again. His lips trembling as he struggled for words. His eyes strictly pierced in my soul. He kept tapping on the desk with his fingers.

'I am seriously very sorry,' he wanted to put me at ease, so he left, like a tornado hitting the edge of my desk.

His pace was magnificent. No sooner had he left, than I picked up my bag and ran out of the office. Gautam was waiting for the lift there. We saw each other while I gaped. For two seconds I stopped and then I took the stairs, letting Gautam in the lift alone. I didn't descend the stairs, thinking of leaving in few moments when Gautam might have left. I waited on the stairs for five minutes before finally going down. As I crossed the front of lift, it opened and Gautam came out. We had already had enough for the day, so this time we ignored each other and went in opposite directions. Both of us were embarrassed.

FRIENDSHIP

While I was on my way to the office there was a bang behind me. I turned in alarm to find Danish, Nahel and Jessica. Among the people I used to hang out with, these were the friends I had made in three years. They were laughing like idiots. There was a funny expression on my face, a blend of surprise and shock. They burst a chips packet near my ear. The security guard turned around in alarm but Danish waved at him to convey that everything was alright.

'What the hell are you guys plotting against me?'

I turned to Nahel and hit his shoulder 'Et tu Brute'.

He hit me back saying 'the lady doth protest too much, methinks' frowning a brow sarcastically.

Nahel was short and sleek. He was often confused for a school student, for which we made fun of him. To tease him, Danish often tried to lift him up which led to a huge fight later.

'Stop killing the essence of Shakespeare, guys.' Jessica pointed a finger at me and Nahel, we burst into a hysterical laughter.

'Amor, I lust after you, don't get me pined. Relieve me of my agony and give me a piece of you.' Danish winked at Jessica, breaking the ice.

They were in love since infancy; on being questioned even they didn't remember the exact moment when they fell in love. Theirs was an era of love. Privately we called them the 'Eraens.' Jessica chirped around Danish's waist and Nahel started whistling, looking at her.

'Drop some of those moves this side too.' I pulled Nahel by sleeves.

'Let's go and have something. It's been days since we had dinner together' I winked at Nahel.

'Oh sure, in all fairness I agree with the lady' Nahel chuckled. I punched him on the shoulder.

'Yes sure why don't we all meet for dinner, right now I got some important work to finish. So we'll meet in the evening.' Danish put an arm around Jessica.

'Roger that.' Nahel and Jessica shouted in unison.

'Nahel and Jessi are you guys busy? If not, let's go to the canteen and have breakfast.'

'I've some work milady. Take this girl with you. You surely seem hungry asking everyone out.' He pushed Jessica while she nearly toppled and hit him.

'I'll come.'

We left while continuing chattering and teasing each other. We went to sit in the cafeteria and ordered coffee and sandwiches. Jessica was whistling and I looked at her in amazement. 'What's wrong with you?

'What's wrong with me?'

'There is something that I wish to discuss with you.'

'What do you wish to say?'

'It's something serious.'

I had thought about discussing it with her, about what was happening between me and Gautam these days, because I wasn't sure if, what I was doing was right or wrong. But I couldn't talk about it to Jessi. I needed time to figure things out.

'What happened? You don't look good all of a sudden, is everything okay?' She peeped through her specs, dressed in a blue jumps suit.

Her curls were falling on her forehead and went further inside her frame;

she had one of the most beautiful curls I had ever seen. The strange sense of dressing made her famous in the entire office but I loved her flamboyant nature. I wished I was a bit like her. I knew if I told her my little secret it would be safe for she was not a blabber mouth.

'I don't know things have been really strange between Gautam and me lately.'

"Isn't he the one to handle your photography team?"

'Yes.'

'What's wrong? Is he creating problems for you?'

'No, no, there is nothing like that. It's just, I... don't know, everything's getting strange.'

'Avisha you can tell me, you know it.' She pressed my hands and comforted me.

'Ok, you know Gautam is a wonderful person. He is a source of inspiration ever since I've known him.'

'Okay, so?' She rolled her eyes.

'So I think lately he has started to give me a strange feeling, I don't know what it is but I feel weird, I don't know...maybe a sense of peace around him.'

'Peace, hmm...Oh, I get it. So something fishy is going on the third floor.' She smiled and winked at me.

'No nothing's going on. This is why I didn't want to discuss it at all. It's all so complicated. It seems like I have an inclination on hurting him by the stubborn attitude of mine.'

'You really think you're stubborn. You are one of the most streamlined people I've ever met, but it's true that the rules you've set for your life, well, they are really tough. You need to loosen up a bit, get out of your shell. And how do you know what you do will hurt him or not? Do you even know how he feels for you?'

'You're right, but it doesn't happen. I think I'm making him fall in love with me and then hurting him at the same time.'

'Okay girl you've got a lot of misconception about yourself here. No one makes anyone fall in love with them, it's not some contract. Secondly, you are not sure whether he loves you or not. You're not a beauty queen that everyone will fall for you. People experiment and they try to look out for potential partners. What do you think; they are going to die one day waiting for you? Wake up girl, even the people who seem inseparable gradually end up with someone else. You'll end up with someone else. We want someone because our happiness lies with them, even if we pretend that we are sacrificing ourselves. So if he is for real, he'll stay. Stop giving it this much thought.'

'I guess you're right and you know you're my best friend, right.'

'You know Danish and I fight almost ten times a day, but even after all these years we're together. You know why? Because we don't believe in an excuse for not making it work. We love each other and everything else is secondary, and trust me, you'll find him, the one who has no excuses but only love to shower. In a way I guess your shell is perfect, and only the right guy will be able to break it.'

'Would he be able to keep aside his insecurities and love me and accept me for the person I am?'

'Don't hallucinate, just let life play its course. Why do you want to be so sure about everything?'

The truth was, I was caught in a dilemma of not wanting it and not willing to lose it either.

Our coffee and sandwich arrived; Jessica took a sip and laid her back on the chair. I looked outside the glass pane and saw Gautam pass. There was a thought in me – Why would I jeopardise his happiness, merely to experiment, or fulfil mine? Jessica was right; 'if he was meant for me he'll stay.'

After the breakfast I hurriedly got up to leave for the meeting. Today Gautam was going to deliver the layout of the trip we had.

'Bye Jessi, I have a meeting today.'

'Bye, I'll stay for a while, Danish messaged his meeting is cancelled so he's coming for breakfast.'

'Okay enjoy and don't kill him.' I winked at her and hugged her before leaving.

After the incident near the coffee vending machine, Gautam and I had started avoiding each other. It was too difficult to pretend that nothing had happened. We had to pretend in front of other people as if we were great colleagues, but, when we were alone we were shy to even look at each other. It was confusing at times, though, for the way I was dependant on him.

'Hello everyone!'

I entered the meeting room and waved hands at Patrick and Kuber. Patrick was the head of the editorial team. He had a huge beard and checked right each criterion on the list of a writer's look. Gautam was sitting at an end and pretended that he didn't hear me. I too was relieved that I didn't have to talk to him. Gradually people started flocking in and Gautam got up to move towards the board. He was in black shirt and grey trousers. I tried not to look at him and instead focused at my notepad.

I have been in love once before and it didn't go well. It was then when I had decided not to fall in love ever. I have never allowed myself to be affected by the idea of emotions and all. That phase of my life was so painful that I thought I would never be able to overcome it. But eventually I did, and the memories faded into nothingness, or in a scar that is left on the skin after a wound. It didn't hurt anymore other than in forms of some nightmares. But when I saw, it was there and the mark reminded me of the very painful wound that had turned today in a painless scar which I never wanted to touch again. What I had faced, I was doing the same to Gautam and making him feel all this, why was I so uncontrollable? Even if I be with him, what was the guarantee that I won't hurt him like I was hurt? Why couldn't God answer my questions?

I was sitting in silence, at times looking at him though pretending to look at the notepad. I was cursing myself for the fact that we were going to Assam, which meant we had to be a team and even if we didn't want, we had to talk as professionals. Gautam delivered the layout of our trip and I took notes with a concentration I never showed before. Gautam was speaking and I heard him, pretending we were just two colleagues. How could I feel all this? I have always believed that I would get what I wanted; how could the purity and intensity of my aspirations become merely an imagination? I felt dragged in the whirlpool of my past again. I wanted a grip on my life while everything went beyond my control. Was I so bad that mere compromises had to become a part of me? I was fighting for my mute thoughts to be heard but the voice came out in silence. I wasn't able to control my tears, so I decided to leave the meeting.

'Excuse me, please.' I whispered to Patrick and pushed back the chair and left, hitting the door. I heard Gautam's fumbling words behind me.

Jessica's words had gone from my mind; I straightway walked towards the washroom, locked myself inside and burst into tears.

I pursued photography for I wanted to get myself out of whatever I had gone through and because I needed a fresh beginning. Gautam reminded me all the more about whatever I didn't wish to think about. He made me want to fall in love again, but I didn't want it anymore. What if I break his heart? I had been in a relationship before and had the share of my life. Now my task was just to build a sound career and marry the man of my parents' chose. My eyes were blood red with tears and suddenly there was a knock on the door. I wiped my tears, my eyes swollen. I washed my face and put on my spectacles, to avoid being looked in the eye. I set my clothes right and left bowing my head so low that no one could look me in the eye.

When I came out my head turned unconsciously to Gautam. I saw him talking to Jiya from 'The Green Horizons' column. She was a newly hired member of our team. She had the Anglo-Indian looks with hazel eyes, loosened brown hairs. He was demonstrating her the arrangement of photographs on the monitor and meanwhile she touched his hands. Though I absolutely had no rights to be mean but I couldn't tolerate that sight

She had to write down an article covering the Assam festival. The article was a major portion of the next edition and she was also accompanying us to the trip. Gautam being the lead of the project was under tremendous pressure. He wanted to cover this article at any cost and I could clearly see the passion in his eyes even from that distance. He was hustling and bustling and noting down every single detail, making data sheets and getting as much help as possible from the past teams that went there. Jiya was leaning on his chair from behind and her chin rested on Gautam's shoulder. Gautam was focused on the photographs while I was studying Jiya's actions. I was anguished at the scene and left in fury because I couldn't stand it anymore. My behaviour was nauseating me. What was I planning on? On one hand I didn't want him; on the other I couldn't see him with someone else.

As I stepped out from the building to get myself a cup of coffee I received a call from Nahel.

'Hi, 'Green Shrubs' it is?'

'Yes sure.' And he disconnected the call.

We unanimously agreed to pay a visit to our favourite restaurant, 'Green Shrubs' and met at six in the evening. The food and ambience was just what we loved. Ample items on the menu, hygienic, but most of all the food was tasty. We often came here but this visit came to life after a long duration as everyone was busy with their schedules. Everyone was free today so we decided to have a fun time tonight.

The attendant guided us to our table, we grabbed a seat each. As soon we entered the restaurant there was a delicate odour of incense sticks diffusing in air and it was so soothing that I realised what I had been missing all these days. A sense of belongingness and calmness towards my being. There was no chair in this restaurant and a jute mat was spread on the floor that gave lap to a low floor table. There were scented candles on the table kept inside red, green, blue and yellow lamps. At a distance there were few artists performing ghazals. The candle flames were smoothly floating in the air, illuminating our faces through the coloured lamps. I wanted Gautam to be around and just look at him the way I did in silence. I missed him deeply and was soaked in his thought when I noticed a couple sitting nearby. They did not utter a word or look at each other, not even got intimate; they were just sitting at each other's side. They looked married. The sense of love was visible. She was laying the plates and he was serving food. She didn't speak anything and neither did he but the synchronisations of their actions were heart-warming. They could anticipate what was going to be the other's next move. It didn't seem mechanical, nor it appeared to be a definite gesture, but the love was evident. People in true love don't show off, but wish it was so easy to hide their love. My eyes twinkled at the thought and I grinned and knuckled Jessica to look at them.

Danish and Jessica were with us and their lives, by then were so entangled with each other that even they didn't know, which part belonged to Danish and which to Jessica. I loved their innocence and that's the beauty of childhood love. You're still chaste and do not loose connection to your naivety and there is always this bridge. Whenever you want to gain your innocence back, remember to walk back to your childhood love. They change, life changes but you somehow find yourself without even expecting to, otherwise there is always this void in which you keep on trying to find yourself; In fact, you lose yourself in childhood. Your childhood is you, rest all is just pretension. No meditation, no self-realisation can let you find yourself. You were your own self, when your mind and heart wasn't veiled or influenced by anything. When you were kids, and first touched by the feeling of love, you were yourself back then.

I drew my attention back to our table after hearing a loud conversation. Nahel was cracked jokes on Jessica and through the blue light reflecting on Nahel's face, Jessica called him 'Avatar'. That was what they always did; they dig up some pseudo name for each other and would fight over it. I had to convince them not to fight. They calmed down too soon and I began feeling lonely again. I felt my physical presence but my heart and mind was somewhere else. I wanted to see him and maybe go and dance with him and calmly rest my head on his shoulder. I did and didn't wish to feel all this at the same time.

Nahel and Danish ordered some chicken drumsticks, barbecue chicken, lemon chicken, fried mushroom buttons and fried cottage cheese. To drink they ordered shakes beers and mock-tails. When the food arrived all of us broke loose on the food. The aroma of food buoyed up in the air defying any gravity and nothing could hold us from eating. I felt guilty about forgetting Gautam for the moment though. My mouth was salivating, and so was everyone's.

While I was sipping my favourite Mojito and Nahel started singing aloud holding his glass in hands. He was a pain in the ass to handle sometimes. The most unpredictable thing about him was his laughter. It was so contagious that once it started it was nearly impossible for him to get rid of it. We looked at him in surprise, when Jessica joined him.

Danish and I smiled at each other at the prospect of forthcoming cyclone in the restaurant. We winked at each other and got up to dance. Two couples already occupied the stage beforehand and glided on the floor. We went to join them.

Danish was a trained dancer. I was not good at dancing but could move a beat or two at my disposal. For some reason, I felt elevated but before I could even start, Danish pulled me by hand and threw me. And then he did all his dance moves experiments on me that he could do with a partner. Ghazal was playing in the background and our dance by no means complemented the music. Our steps seemed more like hip hop but I was still ashamed at how I couldn't dance. I was trying my best to follow his steps when Nahel and Jessica came to join us. Their dance steps were even more hilarious and without any intention they were drawing all the attention to them. The other two couples were looking furiously at us and I passed them a sheepish smile. By now it was too much and Danish pulled Nahel and we changed partners and danced with crazy moves. I could finally shed my inhibitions as I knew there was no way I was dancing worse than these idiots. They laughed like fanatics and I seemed to lose my sense of consciousness. After dancing, I felt relieved in a way. Jessica asked me to get back to the table. The food was still lying waiting to be devoured. Her face was blood red by now and the veins were clearly visible after dancing so much. There was no doubt that everyone was terribly tired and wanted to eat, while Danish and I continued on the floor, Jessica and Nahel went to eat. Danish was teaching me a few salsa steps and the hilarious moment was when the artists stopped performing and some funk song started playing. Though, we were having fun, I felt bad for the artists. So we decided to get back and eat as we were also starving.

As we were descending the podium, I saw Gautam with his friends. I sensed a pinch in my heart as if I had committed some heinous crime. Gautam looked at me in bewilderment. I knew a moment ago I was dancing with Danish and he might have seen me. When he saw me looking at him he got up and left. I felt like going after him to explain what had happened. We have never talked on personal levels, and I wondered what would I tell him anyway? The thought was stupid and even if I wanted, I had no explanations to give, as there was no ground to it. But somewhere inside I loved the way he got angry when I was with someone else. After he left I was anxious for making him mad because I knew for the coming few days I had to bear with his arrogance and ignorance. A thought within my head said maybe he didn't leave because of me, but instinctively I knew why he had left. I ignored it, shook my head and looked at Jessica. She shrugged as if I was blaming her for some crime. I smiled and put an arm around her but lost the appetite to eat.

It was late at night when we decided that we've had enough fun for the day. Danish and Jessica went on his bike, Nahel on his own, while I had something entirely different in my mind. Nahel insisted on dropping me home but I fared him bye and left alone as I lived nearby.

I was passing by Gautam's lane which was nearby but not on my way. I chose to walk past his colony and stopped there staring at his apartment. It was around 2 O' Clock at night and a tea stall was still open. It was a busy road and because it had hostels around, the area was usually crowded, most of them being couples.

'Is he there?' I was lost in thought, when someone kept a hand on my shoulder from behind and I realized where I was standing. It was like I was enchanted by a spell.

I turned to see Gautam there, 'What are you doing here? It's already so late' I could see him read my consciousness, and same reflected in his eyes.

I fumbled for words, eating half of them in my mouth, 'I... I came to uh, I came to drop a friend of mine' somehow the words came out. My heart was thumping loudly, what a jerk I was!

'You're so tough that you came to drop a friend of yours at two in the night?' He was right and I didn't know what to say next. 'I... uh... I... Jessica wasn't well, and she needed me to accompany her.'

'Oh okay, so how will you go back now?

Are you alone?' he said in a cold arrogant tone.

'No, my boyfriend is coming to pick me up, till then I'll walk' these words came out of my mind without me even trying to say it.

'What the hell! Why would I say that?' I asked myself.

'Oh,' Gautam was taken aback. His expressions changed and his face was marked with confusion and humiliation at once.

'Okay, be safe' he didn't even wait for my response and went away with a bolt.

'Why would I say that?' I kept my hand on my forehead.

I knew Gautam was a man of character. He would die but not put himself in a situation that puts him down. My love for him was multiplying in leaps and bounds and heart was beating with thuds. Gautam, his eyes, his words, everything had arrogance tonight. While in aloofness I was rationalising my statement, I saw Gautam return in a bolt to me.

'Why would you do that?' he shouted.

I was taken aback. I didn't expect any of this.

'What did I do?' I mumbled like a sheep.

'Made me believe you love me; drove me crazy all the time. You knew I love you right.' He held my wrist tightly.

I was scared; I never saw Gautam this outraged. His silence, his hesitation, his smell, they were my assets. I held on to them without expecting any more from him.

I looked into Gautam's eyes. It was getting harder to look in them as they demanded justice. I knew I loved him and that I belonged to him but I didn't deserve him. Not even half a quarter. And moreover, my lack of conviction was my greatest weakness, but I was not sure if it was in my control whether to feel for him or not.

His voice got hoarse,

'Avisha...,' and there was silence, '...I love you. I always have. I fell in love with you the day I saw you for the first time. All the small things you have done for me, has driven me towards you. I love you. Avisha, when I saw you dancing with that guy today, I had a tinge of jealousy. Whenever I look into your eyes I find a piece of myself I've never known.' His voice grew softer as he said, and he looked at the ground and shook his head abruptly.

'You love me right?' he said to me and I looked strangely at him suppressing my heart as much as I could.

'I don't. Your arrogance kept me at bay from the day I saw you. I respect you as my teammate and you're an inspiration but I got no feelings for you. I never looked at you in any other way than a colleague. If that laughter, those conversations and meetings meant anything else to you, I am sorry. I am sorry Gautam; I am not in love with you.' I said in the most arrogant tone trying to calm down my heart as much as I could.

He left my wrist shamefully. His face turned red in embarrassment. He shook his head in a strange way.

'Is that it? How could I?' Gleaming through the shimmering light of night, I saw tears in his eyes. He could not hide them, and I could not look at them. He bowed his head low in despair.

'Sorry' he said and turned around walking briskly. I raised my hand to stop him, tell him how much I loved him. When he was around twenty meters away, I found myself running after him. Chasing him; following him where ever he went. He disappeared in a dark lane and I stood restlessly. Tears were rolling down my face and I saw him wipe his eyes, and heard the voice of a man crying. I heard him. I saw him. I cursed me while looking at him. What was I doing? Was I hurting him? Was I hurting myself? I sat at the end of the lane, holding my treacherous heart.

I knelt on the road, whispering to myself – Don't cry Gautam. I love you. Please don't cry. I am sorry. I'm sorry for falling in love with you. I'm sorry for spreading all this pain. I know it's not your fault. It's all me, who has brought you to a point where you can't help yourself. What have I done? I am in love with you. More than you'll ever know, more than I'll ever show. Feel me, look into my eyes. They are yours. You make me alive, you make me live. I wish someday you'd know what you're to me, what you were to me this entire time.'

My heart ached, so did his. What was I doing?

'Gautam,' I kept repeating to myself.

'You're crying there thinking I don't care. Thinking how selfish I could be. I swear it's all a lie. I love you. But, I can't confess it. Not to you, not to anyone. I was always confused if I'm in love with you but this confusion erased all the lines that were between you and me. All the distance that was never supposed to be sufficed, I see it all disappear.'

And then with energy I stood and left from there. I ran, as fast I could. I took a taxi and reached my apartment. Like a paranoid, I unbolted my bedroom's door. Hitting at the edge of bed, tumbling, crying; eyes turning red with tears, I took out my laptop and typed a resignation letter.

I could no longer work at that magazine company; it was all over. What I was doing was so hurtful. Whatever the truth was, be it my love or anything else, I realised that running away, denying something and creating voids won't change the truth and the truth was that I was madly in love with him. The scar was bruised and fresh again, I could feel the pain, and I could feel as if my heart was being ripped out of my chest. He was my strength and I felt frail without him, even if I didn't want to. It was him who gave me hopes, it was him who erased all the pain and made me believe in myself. While I typed each letter, in the resignation, I felt I was committing suicide. I realized without him I was nothing, but ashes.

I was dying. Gautam was dying. We were dying. But something was stopping me. I was hurting and I felt like a culprit. I needed to set my mind clear, but I couldn't. Even if I gave said a yes to Gautam, what if I couldn't be completely loyal to him? I didn't want him to pine for my complete attention or hurt himself. He deserved the best, he must get the best. I wasn't a suitable match for him. God, I was going insane.

I slammed the window hard in an attempt to take my frustration out, leaving it broken. The watchman whistled from below. I waved at him that everything was okay. I bumped on the couch and cried. I cried till my eyes were swollen and sulked with tears.

I cried till I heard the phone ring. 'Hello' my voice was still shaky.

'Hi Avisha, how are you?' it was my mother.

I felt even guiltier. What a pain I was to everyone.

'I am fine, how are you? Why are you calling so late at night?' I tried speaking but she made out I was crying.

'It's long since you called. I called you at least twenty times but you didn't pick up. Where was your cell phone? It's good being a workaholic, but not that you forget your parents right.'

'It's not like that.' I couldn't control my tears so I hung up the phone 'I will call you. I have some work'

'Oh God this girl...' before she could finish her sentence I cut the call.

Strange thoughts came in my mind. Gautam's image was flashing in front of my eyes. His tears, his pain I was to blame for everything. I knew for him, I needed to stop being sceptical. I was the merciless murderer who plotted against his life. With tears rushing down I looked out of the broken window. In a world so big there was no one who could heal me. My aching heart had become an assassin who hunted consecutively on one or another prey.

I choked while crying unable to run away from the maze. I was trapped in. I stood up and started walking briskly. Gautam's face wasn't going away from my eyes. He stood wherever I looked.

If I was in love with Gautam, why couldn't I just confess it to him? It was all too confusing for me. Maybe I wasn't scared of falling in love but scared of losing him. What if he changed, what if the passion died?

What if I didn't love him? Or, did I love anyone other than me? I slipped out of my dress and put on a loose skirt. Then I took out my phone from the bag. I scrolled down to Gautam's number. My fingers rested on the call button. My hands were cold and the wits had gone numb. I looked at his number and thought of calling him to tell him the truth.

I pressed the call button with a pinch in heart only to disconnect the call before it was connected. And tears came in my eyes again as I knew I couldn't do this. I couldn't do this to Gautam. I brought the phone closer to my lips and kissed his name.

'I love you'

I whispered as softly as I could. The whole night I couldn't sleep and lied on my bed thinking about him, thinking how he must be feeling now. At moments I couldn't breathe and there was an intense pain in my heart. Like the ebb and fall of the tides the pain in my heart was playing. I cried the entire night for all the unsaid words that he said today; for manifesting the creation of love in his form, Gautam.

As the night grew darker my pain increased. I got up and stood near the window where the cold wind was hitting my face smashing me. I closed my eyes and allowed the wind to reach my heart. At moments I shivered and opened my eyes smiling. I looked down from my flat's window. The wind was soothing and I missed Gautam. If only he were around the night could have been so much more beautiful. It was full moon and the moon smiled at me reading my thoughts.

I whispered looking out of the window,

'I hate to love you; I hate how badly I want to be around you and tell you I love you. I hate the fact that I can never tell you how much I love you. My love is wrong; you are meant to be mine but I know you'll never be mine. It's not possible for me to love you whom I love so dearly, that I can't even risk losing you. Forgive me for hurting you Gautam, but life has greater assets than love. I can't break your heart. It's not right. I love you, I know that. I tried to deny it so much to myself but I couldn't, and it seems the more time I spend with you, the more I fall in love with you. I love the way you protect me, and take care of me, but I hate the way I am scared of entirely losing you one day. I can't risk you to a relation which tears us apart so badly that our love becomes merely an aching memory.'

Let's just not fall in love. Let's just not confess it to each other.

Denial arouses desire, but let's just kill all desires. Who knows one day we might fall out of love? One day we would laugh at the thought of It.' and I sighed. I took a deep breath. My eyes glinted. I looked into nothingness and shouted, 'Gautam' as he could hear me.

I laughed frantically and tears rolled down my cheeks. I was surprised by my own self. I couldn't control laughing or weeping; both at the same time. What was that? I was in love.

ART OF LOVE

Sluggishly I got out of bed and got ready for office. The resignation letter was resting on the table. I tried to lure myself into believing to forget it there. But before leaving the home I ignored all voices in my head and picked the letter. My strength had already deceived me and every activity was extended by lethargy. I took a taxi and went to the office with a heavy heart. When I reached the building I was confused if I should enter it or not but left everything in the hands of fate and went inside. It was my last day there and I knew that whatever the consequences would be this was the right thing to do. My heart was beating heavily and I felt like a culprit. Howsoever I avoided every time I got up for some work even on taking the biggest precaution I crossed paths with Gautam several times. He smiled at me like a colleague does and the feeling was extremely nauseating. I had never experienced anything that sort before and I felt as a stranger around him. He was indifferent and gave no reaction about last the night. I was in low spirits and every time Gautam passed from my side without noticing me I felt frail.

At times when he passed, I looked in opposite direction. As we came closer I felt a pinch in my heart. Was he was trying to kill me? I raised my hand to stop him in a jerk but realised it was my imagination. Gautam was not even there, he had already gone. I turned around to look at him and not knowing what it was, I knelt on the ground. I cupped my face and sobbed at my agony, I sobbed at Gautam's indifference. He never acted so indifferent in my presence and I have always felt a mystifying force between us. It lacked that day. He was there but his presence was more killing than his absence. I was in love with him but I had closed all doors for him. I was sitting on my desk not working but playing with the resignation letter in my hands. I saw Gautam coming towards me and my nerves went numb. I couldn't imagine what was he going to say? I tried to pretend that I was doing some work but I couldn't concentrate. My eyes were oscillating between him and the papers in nervousness. He walked towards me without any hesitation. As he came closer, he knocked on the desk, 'Avisha' he gave me a smile and handed me a document. He had never given me such a pleasant smile before that day.

'Read it by tonight. We have to get it done so that we could easily head to Assam next week. It's the statistics of the tasks and timelines when the last team went there. We've to perform better than them but also have to adhere to the timelines and guidelines. Please, make a new framework for this trip. And, if you need any help let me know. Although, I think you won't need any, as all the details are clearly mentioned there.' He gave a smile again and left.

I gaped at how distant he had become to me in merely one night. The Gautam whom I saw cry last night had changed in no time. I stared at the document but nothing was visible to me. I felt my whole world demolish in front. My eyes were watery and it felt that Gautam was a total stranger who didn't know me other than being a colleague. I was pushed by an indefinite force and I got up from my seat and went to him, without realising.

'Gautam'

'Yes' he uttered without turning around.

'I am sorry; I can't accompany the team to Assam trip.'

'Okay' that's all what he said. I leaned on a chair as I felt I would fall down. I wanted him to ask me why I wasn't going or shout at me for being irresponsible but he said nothing and didn't even turn around. Gautam couldn't be so rude; He was arrogant, but he loved me or did his heart change in one night. I stood there wanting to say something but what, I didn't know. I wanted him to say something, say anything. While I turned away to leave he said without turning around,

'May I ask why?'

I felt the energy come to me in a flash and instantly answered,

'I am not well and that trip will be quite hectic. I don't think I will be able to handle it.'

It was an excuse; I was holding the resignation letter in my hands which I couldn't hand over to him even after all my resolve. Of course, I was dying to go. I wanted him to pursue me; too long for me. It gave me an uncanny sense of pleasure and satisfaction; hurting him at times. He turned around to look at me; I saw a genuine concern in his eyes.

'Take leave if you wish to. If you feel better in a week you could come.'

I was at once taken by a sense of guilt. How could I hurt him? I didn't know what to say.

'Okay,' I said it and left.

Gautam's eyes were fixed on me while I walked off. I wanted to turn around and confess everything to him: my lies and my love. I was just praying God for a miracle – a miracle that can make him talk and it happened.

He called my name, I stopped and turned but he looked at me vacantly with his glinting eyes and I felt a blush on my face. How did people hide the love behind their eyes? I was terribly weak at this art and Gautam was right; I could never conceal my love and it was always reaching him.

It is so difficult to hide your love from someone you love the most, when you are with them every day and love them so dearly. When the silence lies between the two and they lay so many seeds of hope that reality might fail to fulfil it. You die to tell them what their value is in your life, but you can't, because of the fear that you might lose them. And they blame you that why can't you love them the way they do? Why are you so indifferent to how they feel?

The only answer you can give them is, 'I love you.' But what if then they question, if you love them why can't you express it, or question why your love is so distant? You just can't tell them, all you can say is, 'I wish I could explain.'

You want to tell them how much you love to them, but the fear of what if they don't approve of your love? What if they can't love you back? What if they can't love you at all...? Or, what if they don't love you at all...? There was no hiding from that fact. Whether he was near, or distant, I loved him. At last I had confessed it to myself. It didn't matter now, what I was doing was right or wrong, all I knew was that I belonged to him.

'Will you come down with me for a while?' I saw his lips shiver as he said. His eyes sparkled and few strands of his hair rebelled against the way they were combed.

I stood there dumb struck and tears came rushing down. I stared at him with the eyes of his Avisha. He got up and came closer to me. We walked slowly beside each other, silently, it was a divine feeling. It was difficult to explain how soothing his companionship was. Could anything be so serene, so pure and perfect? I couldn't help but wonder. It was impossible to hide my feelings from him, when I knew he was going away. I felt even weaker bit by bit like life slipping from my hands. Everyone greeted him on the way and I kept walking silently. He was as nervous as I was and I could sense that.

When we reached downstairs, it seemed he wanted to take me out because he headed towards the gate.

"Should we take a taxi?" he asked in a quivering voice.

"I won't mind if you take me on your motor-bike."

I told motor-bike because I just wanted to be close to him for a moment, cherish his company when no one was around. When I could talk to him without the fear of anyone else overhearing us. But, indeed even after trying so hard I couldn't bring myself to make my confession to him. I sat behind him quietly. I tried to speak to him so many times but couldn't, something stop me. Maybe, it was my own weakness that I couldn't translate my thoughts into words and it was getting difficult to hide what I had to say as well as to speak what was going in my mind. Whatever it was I had left it in the hands of God.

He kick-started the bike and we went in a rush. I could see his hands trembling and regretted my decision of coming on a bike with him. He was so handsome and sensible that I wondered where did I stand in front of him? While he was pure and had a beautiful heart, I had only broken pieces of mine. What would I give him anyway?

His left hand had a sports watch and he was in black jeans and green t-shirt. I felt not only lucky but on top of the world to share that moment with him – that unprofessional moment. There were several mustard fields on the way which were perfect scenes for couples to enjoy and have a conversation but he wasn't making any effort to talk to me.

Why couldn't he peep in my heart and know everything? Why did I need to say him anything; anything at all? Couldn't he recite my silence?

Maybe, he did. We went to a quiet coffee shop at the outskirts of the city. He parked the bike and I ran inside to settle my hair. He came inside caressing his hair and there was no length to which I could go to explain his beauty in my eyes. I came in front of him and he got up consciously pulling the chair for me, I felt awkward and surprised. I was not used to this respect by Gautam. He settled in the chair in front of me. There was silence between us.

'We should have something to eat' I tried to ignite scene.

'I am sorry if I made you uncomfortable yesterday,' a reply came with eyes bent low. Though he was fumbling, he tried to speak out something that I was not expecting but it was good that he talked about the last night.

'It doesn't matter.'

'I have never in my life behaved like that. When you come in front of me something just happens; something inevitable.' His eyes got teary.

He withdrew a handkerchief from his pocket and wiped his eye. I didn't expect that. I couldn't see him cry.

'Sorry if I am making you uncomfortable again. When I saw you the first time, I had developed a strange feeling about you. I didn't know if it was love. I don't know yet, if it's love. But it was something I never felt before. I never loved anyone before. Your words have put a silence on me. I promise I won't ever bring this respect to you ever again. But Avisha...' and his throat became sore and he looked in my eyes '...if you can do one thing – don't deny me of your companionship' and he paused 'I need you to be around. For some untold reasons you have to be there. Maybe its love, still, I am not forcing you. Your happiness is what matters the most to me. So, if you feel like getting up and leaving from here, you may. I won't stop you. I understand that I am not acceptable to you.'

I went ahead and held his hands, they were freezing. It was spontaneous. Even I didn't know I was going to hold his hand, not until I had already held them. My heart was overwhelmed. He tried to withdraw his hands.

'Gautam' I took a sigh and held his hands, stopping him. This time I knew what I was doing. I didn't want to let go of him. Not now, not anymore.

'I am not in a relationship with anyone.'

'What?' his head shot up with eyes wide open.

'Let me complete. I don't have a boyfriend. I had one, but it's a long gone story. That's not what's stopping me. I don't want to hurt you I'm not sure unto what point I'll be able to be with you. I am scared that one day either of us will change, one day I'll end up hurting you. I don't wish to ruin anyone's life.'

'You won't ruin mine,' he whispered, 'I have seen it in your eyes.'

'Goddamn it Gautam, why don't you understand it. These are the eyes of a betrayer. Look into them. They can do nothing but betray you. Have mercy on your heart. Go Gautam, and choose someone who deserves you, who is sorted because I'm scared of commitments now. I am messed up. I might end up messing your life as well. And what are you thinking I might change?'

I looked away and laughed sarcastically,

'A born devil dies devil, nothing can change me.'

I turned around and said coldly,

'We just don't fit together, and you and I are two pieces that can never be a part of the same puzzle. Don't punish yourself by being with me. Go, live your life. The woman you have worshipped for so long has worshipped you besides everything. But, you are God Gautam, while I am the devil.'

I wept and said. Gautam stared at me.

'Avisha, I could never gather the courage to talk to you till last night. I thought I had lost you. I didn't know how to confront you today. The only thought in my mind was why had I told all those to you. That, you might not even talk to me. I tried so hard to hide myself behind the veil of professionalism. Walking in front of you today was the most difficult thing I have ever done in my life. You wouldn't know how I feel; to protect and preserve you. Avisha, decide what you want, but do me a favour. Let me take care of you. Don't love me back. But, let me love you. This is the only feeling that has been completing me since I saw you. My life before that was a barren desert. After meeting you, if not for you, I don't know what else I will live for.'

His eyes were still looking at the floor. I could see no happiness in his eyes that I was not with anyone; that, I didn't belong to anyone else.

I could see he didn't want me. He truly and sincerely needed me. His eyes had only purity.

'And what if I end up hurting you one day?'

'Don't you see you're scared of hurting me, isn't that proof enough that you don't want to? Who knows about the future? As long I'm here, we'll make it work. If and only if, you allow yourself to trust me, if not love...'

'It's for you to decide. Anything you say today, I will accept it as a command.' I whispered looking at our hands united in one.

'I love you' his tears fell on my palm. I didn't say anything. 'I love you' he said again. He looked at my hands holding his. His grip tightened.

There was a silence, and he wept like a child. The strong man, who protected everyone wept. I couldn't control my tears.

How could I feel that pure? I caressed his head, crying and looking at him.

'You don't even know what you are for me. I have never felt this weak and strong at the same time ever in my life, as in your presence,' he whispered silently. Everyone stared at us while we both cried without uttering a single word, holding each other's hands.

PETITE JOURNEY

Gautam was walking ahead and I followed his footsteps accompanying him to the woods. No one knew that we were in love and we in a way hadn't confessed it to each other. I didn't know where he was taking me as I was plainly walking on his footmarks.

I was happy and sacred, I could see, so was he. He was silent and after around half an hour he asked me to stop. I spotted a dry tree and touched its coarse trunk as I rested my back on it. I took out a book from my bag and started reading it, as he lied on a broken tree's branch. The sun was dim and the frigid air was piercing my body. I was amazed by how beautiful the whole surrounding was; being with him; alive with him. I brought a flask of coffee and we poured one cup each, *'Moments are what we make them, and love is what we believe in. It's love that grows us, it's love that binds. So if today there are moments that you think you can deny, you must try to appease your soul, but the truth will come out and only the truth will stay, rest all will fade and shall fade, for only then you can cherish the truth when you've known the lies.'*

'What are you saying?'

'I'm reading to you, listen to me.'

'Okay.'

'The purity of heart seeks only for purity, and nothing shall ever deny the purity of the other. The dirt will leave, the filter of love will clear the spots and your life shall shine again, only if you believe' and I looked at him, I looked into the book again,

'There are moments when your heart will decide to choose the lies and leave what the truth tells you. Even in the face of the greatest adversities you must stick to the truth, because if you overcome the fear you will reap

unexpected rewards. Never betray your love; never betray the one who loves you, both are equally grave crimes. But never force love on anyone, if they chose to go let them fly, for it means that your love lies somewhere else.'

'I don't get you.' He said.

I kept reading. *'Never blame someone for not loving you, love can't be forced as an artificial tree, but only be grown when you plant a seed. I'll never force my love on you. If it grows I'll know it was real, if it doesn't I'll know I don't deserve you.'*

'What are you talking about – plant, trees, force and all? My truth is you, I'm in love with you, can't you feel that?' I closed the book and looked at him while he looked back at me.

I talked nonsense escaping his eyes and said continuously. He smiled and looked at the ground and lifted his eyes again. He gestured me to come near him to show me the pictures he clicked that day in Mysore. I was surprised that he still had those pictures. I didn't want to get up and see the pictures so I looked at the ground and pressed my lips. He looked away in some other direction and kept back his camera, 'Let's go shooting.'

There were several birds chirping at a distance and the weather was stinging my spines. The coffee gave me gooseflesh with every sip. There was a beautiful smile on my lips and it felt I was living in some other world.

'What happened?' Gautam asked.

'Some crazy ideas, not much...' I broke from the thought.

'Tell me' he asked again.

'I can't seem to describe the mental image I have, so let it be. It's not even an important thought.' I said observing his inquisitive eye.

That mysterious sensation had given me relief making me beam for no specific reason. And I couldn't add up what the thought was. He rose from the branch and walked to me. I was clueless about what to say to him. His gait was enchanting. It was so refined that when he walked it appeared to me as a pull towards him. Like every step that he took was calculated and each time he looked at me, his sight was left lingering there with snapshots embedded in the sheet of air. He was in a blue jeans and blue t-shirt. As he came near, he asked me a question settling next to me.

'I have a question in my head?' he said noticing the branch he just got up from.

'Yes?'

'That day when you saw me around the coffee machine why did you run away.'

'I don't know. What do you think?' I smiled at him.

'You know, I so wanted to leave and not act like that. I have never acted in such a strange manner in my entire life. You, the culprit, have made me a crazy man you know.' He laughed still looking at the branch.

Then he looked at me, and removed a strand of hair that was falling on my face, tucking it behind my ear. He stared at me, and though he didn't speak a word his eyes did all the talking.

'Let's go.' he got up.

We got up to leave and he looked at me and walked silently. After about ten minutes, he asked me to stop. I didn't speak anything and froze where I was, resting my arms on the twig of a tree. He came behind me and I heard his feet crushing the dried leaves beneath his feet. He asked me not to move and gently moved closer to me from behind. I stood silently marked by confusion that what was on his mind. He took out his handkerchief, it was grey in colour. Gently he placed his hands over my eyes and whispered, 'Close them.'

With the adeptness of a priest he tied the knot of handkerchief behind my head covering my eyes. The smell of a freshly washed handkerchief with a musk perfume on it hit me. My eyes were covered and I couldn't see anything. I heard him walking again in front of me and he said softly holding my hands,

'Follow me.'

I was already paralysed leaving all my control to his commands. It was a numbing sensation that his hands were holding mine, in a tight grip. I couldn't act the same way as he did. I walked guided by him and touched by his calmness. Everything else other than him was a lie. It's a true saying, 'Silence is golden.' About ten minutes later, he stopped. He asked me to not open my eyes until he told me. I could hear a loud noise of water falling. My heartbeat was racing. I did as he said. He untied the handkerchief from behind and asked me to open my eyes.

When I opened my eyes, I saw a mesmerising view in front that made me almost faint for a while in excitement. The sun was glistening in front of my eyes and there was a waterfall. We were looking through the window of a small hut. There was a beautiful flower lawn. Dahlias, Hydrangeas, small flower beds were mowed. One apple and litchi tree was swaying in the wind. There were two chairs kept in the lawn. There was a huge pine forest on the other side of waterfall which at a distance of around fifty meters was uniting with the sea. We were standing near the delta. I looked inside the hut; it had a small table on which few candles were kept. There was a wet smell of woods and it was cold inside. There was nothing else in the room.

I blinked my eyes and pinched my hands. It was not a dream, but at the same time it was too good to be true. I was mesmerised. I turned to look at Gautam and he clicked a photo as soon I turned. He looked in the camera, and pretended it was nothing special he had done for me. He pressed his lips like a little child who does so after doing some mischief.

I took the camera from his hands and clicked his photo. He stared at the camera and tried to take it from me. I moved in another direction while he attempted to snatch it again. I was finding delight in teasing him. He was fighting to get it back. I was not letting him touch it. While he was struggling, I laughed my heart out.

'Don't do anything with my camera?'

'Why? It's my life, give it back.'

'What if I don't?'

'I know you'll give it back to me.' He smiled.

'Does it matter more than me?'

I hung the camera out of the window. He leapt to grab it. My left hand was outside the window. I was laughing, teasing him. Gautam's body touched mine and he got hold of the camera. A shot of voltage travelled in my body. I let loose the camera. My hands opened automatically. In an electrifying moment, I grabbed his waist. He let the camera fall in the lawn. Gautam leaned on me. I could feel his breath. It was a misty moment. His perfume was mesmerising. I could anticipate his thoughts? When I could not stop myself any further I hugged him. He removed his hands from the window and put it behind my waist. We gave in the moment. He took me away from the window and we danced. I kept my hands on his shoulders, and he kept his hands on my waist. We moved to the music of the waterfall. I loved the way he guided me. I lacked the art of dancing, and he laughed at my ignorance.

I rested my head on his chest. 'How were you dancing that day with Danish?' I punched his stomach, and he held me tighter.

'Dance with me like you never did? Feel the rhythm of my heartbeat. No one has felt it before. It's only for you.'

He swirled me like a top. We swayed.

'Do you love me?'

'Yes...' I whispered.

'Do you love me?'

'Yes...' I answered again.

'Do you love me?'

'Yes,' and after a pause I said, 'I love you.'

He pulled me closer. We danced to the rhythm of the waterfall.

'Truly...?'

'Yes...'I cried, 'I love you' and looked in his eyes. He hugged me. I felt I would break in his arms. I hugged him back. I felt alive in his arms. He possessed me entirely.

'I love you' I sobbed

'Promise me you will never go away from me?'

'Never, not until I die. Even after my death, I will stay with you. If you won't be there my body and soul, neither can breathe. You mean everything to me.'

'Don't say this. You will never die. You will live forever. Forever, even after the earth ends.'

'Really...?' he looked at me and laughed.

I made the crying face of a child, and he laughed again and hugged me. After dancing for a while, we went out.

The breeze was chilling and soothing. Gautam went and picked the camera. We went to see the waterfall. It was an awe-striking view. At the side of the waterfall there was a small pond and ducks were taking a swim.

'How did you get to know of this place?'

'My mother used to bring us here when we were young. We came with our maternal aunt and their family.'

'Oh, so you are trapping me.'

'Well, I am thinking of' he smiled at me.

'I am not that easy to get.'

'Who wants to get you? I just want to 'be with you' as long I live.'

I was left speechless. We held hands, while the waterfall poured down splash of happiness, deep into the sea.

NOSTALGIA

Gautam asked me to meet his family. Though, I had already seen them in studio sometimes, I have never had the courage to talk to them. I always wanted to know them. His family had an elegant element that was rare even in the most prestigious people. It was just her mother and sister who visited.

When Mrs. Sharma used to bring lunch or dinner for everyone, they used to lick the last morsel off their fingers. Mrs. Sharma had passed me a smile many times and I returned her smile with comfort every time. Gautam was exactly like her, laid back and relaxed. When he walked around he oozed protection in his surroundings. No one could avoid his presence. He was a perfectionist and I was just the opposite, just a clumsy girl. We were the last pair on earth that could fall in love. But, strange as it may seem, after meeting him I found myself changing. The better word to describe is, 'transforming.' All my roads ended on him.

He often fed me with his hands. His family stayed here while I belonged to Dehradoon so he brought lunch from home for me too sometimes.

He loved non-veg and I was a pure vegetarian. I loved reading, he hated it. Photography was an escape for me, while it was his passion. I was tough with people while he could gel with them as he knew them since ages. I could not step out in sun while he didn't mind roaming out howsoever bright the sun might be. He loved rain and was crazy about it, I hated rain. Somebody once said, opposites attract.

I was nervous and lost in his thoughts in my apartment wearing a plum colour dress. My open hair was greeting the wind as I stood near the window waiting for Gautam. Today was a very big day for us. I was going to meet Gautam's family. Meet them, as his beloved. I knew them, but was sure they would know me only if Gautam showed them some photograph of mine. I held a coffee mug in my hands and was praying to God to give me some strength. Gautam had never been to my flat. I wondered what was taking him so long.

I picked my phone to call him. As I was about to dial his number the doorbell rang. I was happy that he arrived. I ran to the mirror to take one last look at my resemblance and then went ahead to open the door.

I was shocked as I opened the door. It was Vivek, the neighbour who used to drink and beat his children every night. He often tried to create nuisance knocking at my door. His was love marriage and he cursed the day he decided to get married.

I held the door as he nearly toppled on the floor.

'Hi Avisha' He said and regained his balance while I looked at him in confusion.

'What are you doing here?'

'I am sorry to have come like this.'

'What are you doing here?' I repeated the question emphasising each word. Suddenly I saw his wife storming from inside her home, 'I am divorcing him. Today he nearly killed our son. It's enough. It's enough.'

'I can't live without you,' He turned to her and said.

'It doesn't matter now. You should've cared about this before creeping up with insecurities.'

'Don't say it.'

'It doesn't. This marriage is over.'

'Please don't say this.'

'We are no more together; I would prefer dying alone than being with you.'

'You're being rude Sapna,' he tried getting closer to her, while she moved back. It was like a movie, I tried to explain them to go back and argue in their apartment because the fight was so heated up that it was wise not to interrupt.

'I loved you so dearly. You always questioned my love. I am sorry for the feelings which are now gone, there is only a sense of void left. Forgive me, but I don't love you anymore.' She wiped her tears and moved towards the lift with her son and daughter, and a luggage.

'I know I couldn't fight my insecurities, but now I am ready. I fell weak and I know I hurt you. Alcohol is just a way to hide the weakness, but I promise from today onwards I won't ever touch it. Forgive me. Avisha please help me.'

I gaped and tried to say something when she pointed me a finger, 'Stay out of it.'

I realised that it was better for me and thanked her in silence.

'Vivek, I won't judge you as a person. I am sorry I just can't be connected to you like that anymore. It doesn't come from within so please let me leave peacefully. My life is not a joke where whenever you want you come, you do and say sorry and expect me to keep loving you like I'm your mother. I could have loved you like that if only you had little respect to see how I was trying to make this relationship work; how I'm carrying the entire load alone on my shoulders while all you're doing is trying to find an escape. You've to fight for us, to earn us a living, you've to realise that when someone loves you unconditionally it's not an obligation, it's just their love. I could have stayed for you, but you know what, these kids have no fault to deserve a hostile life each day. I don't know how they will turn out in future but for now, they deserve a safe and normal life.'

'Sapna...'

'You have erased all that love from within me. No words, Vivek, mind it. No words can ever make me love you the same way and yes, learn to stand up to your insecurities. The next time we'll talk it will be through my lawyer.' He got up to go near her. She moved few steps back; he couldn't say any other word. Her voice got heavy, like she would break down then and there.

'I don't blame you. You were there in this heart. I waited for you to say. –

'I surrender Sapna, forgive me, my life is yours' – but I can't anymore. It's my trust that's broken. You've changed; this alcohol has made you someone I never knew.'

'I am here because I love you,' He toppled moving towards her.

'Does it matter anymore, no it doesn't?' She said and kept the luggage on the lift and moved inside with her kids.

She pressed a button and the door of the elevator closed. I didn't know what to say to him then. He left. I was surprised at how she was so indifferent to him and how indifferent he was to her, that she left and he let her go letting their marriage fall apart. How did they stay together or why did they waste their times over each other if it had to come to an end like that, where they lost total respect for each-other? It was strange. And what's even stranger was that people keep falling in relationship, with one, two, three or even more people. Why do they fall in love and bear all the suffering with the wrong one when they can straight away find the real love of their lives? It didn't matter. God must have thought something. Sometimes they say it all happens so that when you meet the right person, you know how to cherish them. But what about the innocence, does it stand on any ground when you decide with your mind and not heart. Maybe it does, neither I am an expert on the subject nor do I wish to become. I just wanted one thing that no one ever feels any pain of betrayal because it breaks you in ways that only the one that goes through it can understand. The pain isn't just worth it. It's a total loss of emotions when you repeat them over and over again, until you reach the point when your need is given the name of love and when your love is but your need. Even their words didn't reach each other, let alone their silence. Vivek and Sapna scared me for sure. Was it too soon to meet Gautam's family? I went to look at my phone. There were five missed calls from Gautam. I called him back. Someone patted on my shoulder. It was him. He had entered through the open door.

'Where were you? I had so much trouble finding your flat?'

He said to me in a whisper looking concerned. I hugged him. He held me and wiped my tears.

'What happened?' he looked in my eyes.

I shivered as I cried. He kissed my forehead and said, 'Tell me what happened?'

I told him everything and sobbed.

'So why are you crying? Did they do or say something to you?' he asked.

'they just let their marriage fall apart. But, I couldn't. I couldn't. I couldn't accept the fact that those people could be so indifferent to each other. Are relationships so easy to break, that people just leave one person in pain and move on? How do people become so insensitive?' I looked at the floor confused if it was all real and if I was stupid to tell all this to Gautam.

'This is all that you've learnt from them? Are you growing sceptic of me?' Gautam said with a sore throat.

'Gautam I can't lie to you. I can promise you one thing, I will never lie to you. I will never let you break. I will never let you repent your decision of being with me.'

Gautam laughed at my statement.

'Oh, you don't have to worry about me. You know when I saw you I saw a baby who needs to be loved and Avisha; I am not here to possess you. I am not here to keep you. I am here to be with you, just be with you. Don't worry about anything. You feel you are not pure but it's your purity that has pulled me to you. Love me, or don't it can't stop me from loving you,' he held my face in his palms.

'I don't care Gautam. I know only a pure heart like yours can love people without expecting anything from them. And, I feel if I were even one percent of what you are I would be blessed, but people I've known have shaken the roots of love, that I religiously believed in.'

'You know, why she went away from him. Why he left her crying? Because as per today's definition for love; all people want to do is possess. The person that wants to possess anyone they have, how can they selflessly love anyone at all? Or how can they love at all? Avisha, if you were not pure you must not be speaking the truth to me now. Love is giving freedom, because when you leave something free it always returns. When you try to bind someone they'll always leave. Imagine for a while you are tied with a diamond rope to stand near a golden castle, you'll enjoy the view for a while and then eventually get bored of looking at the same castle every day because it will be monotonous to look at. But if you're allowed to walk free, you'll go and see the beautiful monuments of world and appreciate the beauty of the castle in its own way. Beauty is not present in bondages but in freedom. I've seen the kind of freedom you've in your eyes, the desire to soar that you possess and I'll let you soar, because I want to see your world Avisha, I want to fly with you in your world.'

'I don't know how you see it in me, but I have lost the power to see any good in me anymore.'

'You know why, because you are scared of being betrayed; you are scared of losing my love and belief from within your heart. But, love is never lost. It's covered in a layer of dust but it never leaves you. The intensity of love you can feel is not what I or anyone else can make you feel, it's what is within you, I can just make you aware of it. When fear comes in existence, love is shadowed. As for me, you are my child, and my mother. I have surrendered myself totally to you. I am your father and your child. This is how I will spend my entire life with you. This is how I will love you. If you feel you have lost your purity. It's only because you don't feel the true love. True love is pure, Avisha. You will get it, get it entirely from me. Don't worry; I won't leave you ever. I love you.'

I didn't know what to say to Gautam. All I could do was just stare at him in surrealism, with opened eyes. Don't show me these dreams Gautam, and if they'll break I won't be able to live.'

'I won't be able to live if your dreams break, they're mine just like you are.'

I silently cried with an overwhelming heart. Whoever I trusted until then, wanted to possess me only, I didn't know what made him crave for me. What purity he saw in me that I wasn't aware of?

'You take rest today. You can come to my house some other day.' My head was resting on his chest. I raised my face and said, 'I want to go now.' He smiled and placed a kiss on my forehead.

'Are you sure?'

'Absolutely yes.'

'By the way your home is well decorated,' he caressed my head. I knew he was lying because it was all a clutter.

'Really, do you like it?'

'I love it.'

'Seriously...?'

'Yes, but not more than you do.'

'Gautam...'

'Yes'

'I am nervous to meet your sister and mother.'

'They already know you. I talk so much about you...'

'You talk to them about me? Are you insane...?'

'Yes, lately you have been the hot topic of discussion at our home.'

I looked at him and smiled.

'It's getting late. We must go now.' I got up.

'Wait...' Gautam held my hands and got up after me.

'What?'

He came near me, and took me in his arms. I felt his grip on my wrist. He held my hands behind my waist; tied them with his hands. I looked at him surprisingly.

'What?' I asked him.

'Say something.'

'What?'

'What's the capital of Australia?' He made an angry face. I laughed at him.

'Ah, Delhi.' I made an innocent face.

'Oh, with pleasure. I am not taking you anywhere.'

'I love you,' I said immediately and he smiled.

'It pacifies me. Keep saying it as long our souls exist.' He whispered.

I submerged my face in his bosom. We descended the stairs and he leapt to cross each stride. I hated to take the stairs. I wished I had some other choice because in anger Vivek had broken the lift button.

AUTUMN

We were hardly together for a week and it almost seemed like a dream but that was the best part. Everything real, whether good or bad seemed to be like dreams until a substantial duration of time passes in it. I was amazed at how pretty the course of life had turned into. It was an exhausting day for both of us. Today we had to wrap up lot of deadlines and at the same time had to visit his home at night. I wanted to be surrounded by him all the time but knew it was not possible for the day. Even when he was not around, he was always somewhere near me. His presence was far too real for me to accept. By the end of day, both of us were totally wasted and had no energy left for anything. But there was a bigger call that we needed to attend to and had no good reason to avoid it. It was funny that while I was shattered in pieces not more than half an hour ago Gautam had taken me aback by his usual gestures. I didn't know if it was real or a dream but I knew, I had all of him to myself in that moment, and he had all of me to him. While I was lost in thoughts, Gautam pulled the car in a corner. I was surprised.

'Have we reached?' I was surprised for we were still in the midst of market.

'Not so soon lady, relax!' And he jumped out of the car.

'Where are you...?' Before I could advance my sentence, he was gone.

I waited for him and turned on the radio. Some old songs were broadcasted, one of which my mother loved. I smiled at the memory of it. I remembered how my mother fought with dad to buy that cassette one night when we were returning from a movie. I loved my father and mostly for his childlike behaviour. Of all the seasons he loved rainy season the most. He would watch television or read newspapers sitting in the balcony with tea. My mother would insist him to go on a drive. He would avoid it most of the times. But whenever we went on a drive he always made sure we had ice creams. I couldn't help but smile upon those memories.

There were times when we were retuning on the scooter and I would fall asleep and she would hold me while I sat between her and dad. On reaching home, even before they could open the door properly, I would run inside to fall on the bed and sleep. Then, dad used to come and take off my shoes and kiss me on the forehead. Those memories were too precious for me to trade for anything. I wished if I could turn back in time and release my past that was tied in chains all over again.

During nights, when the temperature was low, I would be sheltered under a quilt for as long as I wasn't engulfed in the arms of sleep. Life was so simple and beautiful. But then, when I thought of Gautam it felt like this present was equally precious to me. It was no different than my childhood when I was with him. I had the same sense of innocence, same carefree attitude when he was around. He knew how clumsy I was when it came to taking care of myself, and I knew how clumsy he was when it came to taking care of himself. I wouldn't trade it for anything. I felt owned and consumed by him. Life with him at times felt like a dream to me. Every small action of his was filled with love, care and affection. If life had to be tough on me, so that one day I could be with him in peace, I could bet I would have taken any amount of pain to keep him around and feel his love.

Mentally I had told him a thousand times how much I loved him before I actually told it to him. That is when someone knocked on the door. I was shocked, and my heart jumped a beat. It was Gautam,

'What...? Are you planning to kill me?'

'Not so soon,' he leaned on the door.

'Where did you go?' my eyes framed a surprising look on them.

He brought his hands forward. There was a bouquet of red roses. I smiled at him. 'What is this for...' a pleasant smile turned on my lips in a reflex.

'Uh...just to see your smile' he winked at me.

'When will you stop surprising me?' though delighted I was being formal.

'Oh, see I have just met you. I want to capture your smiles. It's like my second job, other than the one I get paid for.'

We laughed at his statement. He moved to the other side and opened the door of the car and sat on the driver's seat. He took out his phone from his pocket and kept it on the dashboard before he started driving. My heart was beating loud, all his activities were similar to that of my father's.

'Gautam?' I left an inquisitive question mark after my statement.

'Yes' he turned to look at me.

'How far are we from your home?' I asked nervously.

'Come-on, relax. I am there. You don't have to worry. I will take care of everything, just be yourself. And if at any point you feel uncomfortable, just let me know. We will leave from there.'

'No, but still, how far are we...?'

'Ten more minutes. See your comfort really matters here.'

'I mean they are your family'

'Oh, yes. But ma'am...' he made a funny face and looked at me, '...see I am your slave so I have to run your errands.'

I laughed at his statement. 'you are my slave. Accepted. What about me being your mistress from the moment I saw you?'

I leaned towards him and spoke looking out for his reaction.

'Oh were you, really?' his brows frowned.

'Yes. Or the question should be, are you?' I smiled in an obvious manner.

'Okay, so are you?' Seriously...?' I teased him.

'Well yes, in my notion.' He shrugged and looked at me,

'You're my family.'

I looked out the window and there was a herd of sheep passing by in the forest. The car was emerging a dense cloud outside as the temperature had dropped below as it was the year end. Though, the blower in the car made it relaxing and cosy as long we were inside but mostly because he was there. There was a mild smell of oranges diffusing from the bottle of freshener. Gautam's perfume was reaching out to me and I had a sense of comfort disguised by the feeling of being laid back.

There were many moments when our eyes met and both of us identified what was going on within us but it was a prohibited area and no one indulged to talk about it. Or, better no one had enough courage to do so. It was too difficult to change the topic, even more difficult to stay on the same.

Gautam was of a traditional mind-set. At times it felt like we were manufactured in some other era, and delivered in some different era. Both of us loved each other exactly the way we were. And it was strange how similar our thoughts were. However, our actions were just the opposite. When I was happy, and out of my gloomy disposition, I would act like Gautam and feel him beating inside me. Sometimes when I dressed for the sake of deliberate dressing, looking beautiful and Gautam was not around I felt his presence inside me. I would look in the mirror, and it was strange but I could find him peeping within me, as if it was not me but him. Along with this, I had a surge of power within me. I felt at peace as the thought engulfed me in its arms, that sense of my womanliness was already materialised, that, I was no more a creation of my complexities but a carving of Gautam's love.

There were times when we were not together during the meetings, when he was into something else but even through the distance I could guess what was on his mind, what he felt, how he felt. I knew there had to be a veil between us but strangely there was none. He would act in a way I wanted him to when I hadn't said a word to him. He read my silence or maybe he owned my soul more than he should have.

Most of the time I had to bear with his arrogance. Maybe because of the way he felt or maybe the way he was shy about the feelings he had which he could neither express nor hide. It was always better to ignore by not talking or avoiding as I didn't exist. But the strange fact was that I never felt offended by him no matter how rude he was and I always felt so loved around him.

I loved it when during the meetings he would concentrate looking at others and meanwhile I could look into his eyes. There was a charismatic smile on his lips that fluctuated as he went on with the meeting. I knew it was all too much to imagine but the sense of peace that I felt in his presence latched me to him. When I was around him it seemed not loving him was a sin though loving him was also a sin. Not loving him was a greater sin as if God wanted me to love him. It could have all been a manifestation of my delusional mind until the point I knew that he loved me more deeply than I could ever imagine.

While I was lost, my head instinctively turned to him and he was looking at me.

'What's it about?' I asked him, there was a mild smile resting on his lips.

He nodded his head, 'Nothing.'

'Tell me,' I asked him with my head rested back on the seat.

He moved his hand closer to mine and caressed my cheeks and said, 'I love you.'

I tenderly shifted on my seat and kept my head on his shoulder. His smell was mystically soothing and it felt like I had everything I could wish for. Life, before then, never had a sense of satisfaction that I could feel in his belongingness. We stayed silent all the way. I closed my eyes and the light played on my eyelids. I sensed the shadows casting and leaving without opening my eyes. He stopped the car when we reached. My heart started pounding.

'Get down here, I have to park the car.'

I wanted to meet his family but I couldn't muster the courage to get down of the car. I was a rookie in that moment and I wanted him to lead me. I was quiet like the hills.

'What happened? Don't worry, it's your own house.'

'… but this is the first time, I'm scared.'

'Just give me two minutes, let me park the car and then I will take you inside holding your hands.'

That was what I wanted to hear. I knew he was someone who wouldn't leave me alone at any point of time. My blood had almost turned cold when I got down from the car. I stood there to settled my dress and waited for him to reach me so that he could introduce us to each other. My nervousness was obvious and at that point of time nothing could alter my feelings because to feel something is different but to reach that situation in reality it becomes something entirely different.

BLANKETED

His mother was sitting in the portico. As soon as I saw her, I stood there frozen. As I was growing up I was imbibed with several manners but currently I seemed to forget all of them. I walked forward and greeted Mrs Sharma. I had seen her earlier several times but today it was so intentional, that even on trying I couldn't put my nervousness aside. Gautam returned after parking the car and smiled at me us. My eyes oscillated between him and her. He looked at me indicated to move further to meet her. I closed my eyes, took a deep breath and pressed my lips before putting on an elated smile. I respected her through the momentary encounters we occasionally had.

She came towards me in an off-white silk sari. It had a golden border, her spectacles were resting on her nose and a crystal bead strand was hanging from its edges and connected both sides – it looked like a necklace from behind. She looked elegant. I wondered if I would ever look like that. As she came closer to me, her smile made me reciprocate. Today for the first time it seemed like I knew her from ages. While I was about to raise my hands to greet her she hugged me. I widened my eyes and looked surprisingly at Gautam resting my chin on her shoulder. He smiled and shrugged. She parted from me and caressed my head.

'Gautam, I know what you saw in her' she bowed her head and looked at him through the gap above her spectacles. Gautam blushed while I was too embarrassed to say anything. Gautam accompanied me inside the house. It was a beautifully decorated house full of greenery. The interior was cosy and warm, and there were lots of bonsai plants in every possible space of the room. The room smelled of a plant nursery. The plants were welcoming and I felt at ease immediately. The house was decorated by Gautam's mother. Everything kept in the room seemed to define its own space and integrity. Like all that existed in the house had an importance and nothing was out of place. Whatever was occupying the house or its surrounding seemed to be the righteous owner of its area. I felt nervous at her brilliance and at the same time, I feared the uncertainty that I would be able to take care of the house like she did. She certainly was an angel. Shreya stepped out all of a sudden. I was delighted to see her. She looked even more familiar to me than Mrs. Sharma.

'Hi, miss colleague!' she said and winked Gautam an eye. I pressed my lips not knowing what to say. Gautam was laughing in the corner.

'What? Have you met her before?' his mother said.

'No, but the way he has described her, it does not seem that she is any stranger to us?' I couldn't help my laughter.

'Oh' Mrs. Sharma gave me a look that embarrassed me.

'Avisha, you are like my own daughter. Obviously, you must not be as notorious as her. Still, just feel at home, and don't be so shy, you barely speak.' And she put an arm around my shoulder. I looked at Gautam and he shrugged again.

Shreya came to me and pulled me by my hand. I followed her and she showed me the house and talked a lot. I could make out that we were going to be great friends, given, the fact, that I loved babbling myself only to my friends. It was just as long as I was formal with her, I was quiet, after that, I knew how crazy we were going to drive Gautam. In few minutes Gautam joined us. We went at the backyard and she showed me the trees that Mrs. Sharma had planted. They had a collection of trees and plants from all across the world and Mrs. Sharma took care of the trees like her own children, or even more than them, in Shreya's words.

Shreya was three years younger to Gautam and one year younger to me. She was a beautiful girl with an innocent face and was fairest in her family unlike Gautam or Mrs. Sharma so I could make out she must look like her father. I wanted to ask Gautam about him but could never gather enough courage to land in a territory that had mines laid all over it. I didn't want to burst a single one to hurt him. So, we walked in the lawn while I noticed whatever she showed me.

It was a beautifully mowed lawn and I couldn't resist myself from admiring the house. We settled in the chairs kept over there and Shreya ran inside and got some old albums and started showing the photos of Gautam and the family to me. I felt alive. Like I belonged there and it was my home. Mrs. Sharma was also looking at the album and briefed the pictures to me. After showing the pictures, we broke a means to start a small talk.

'Are you comfortable?' she asked.

'Yes, absolutely.' I tried to answer as decently possible.

I felt a surge of life in me. There were elements that I always missed in my family. Maybe it was the display of love. The sense of inadequacy, that I was all alone, in myself. And, that, I had to take care of myself, or just hold back, being tough on myself. It was all bizarre but the moment I came here, I felt at ease. She got up to go to the kitchen to get something to eat.

'Shreya,' Mrs. Sharma called her inside.

'I'm Coming' she said and rolled her eyes before going inside.

With love in my eyes I looked at Gautam. He was blushing like a girl. I held his hands and they were cold.

'I love them,' I whispered.

'And me...?' he raised his face smiling like a child.

'I love you,' and I held his hands tenderly.

'Really...?' the grip of my hands tightened his wrist, and I rested my face on my other hand supported by table.

'Yes' before I could say anything else Mrs. Sharma returned with coffee.

The weather was getting colder so we decided to move inside. Gautam turned up the heat of blower and the blood in my body appeared to melt with the heat, there was an instant sense of relaxation.

'The coffee is delicious' I said after taking the first sip.

'Oh, it's just a demo.

'Ask this fool to prepare coffee for you sometime. Today I have to save his dignity, else I would have asked him to prepare it,' she said while I was staring at Gautam all this time. He raised his collar like some Hercules.

'Do you?' I asked him.

'Well you must decide that for yourself,' he said.

'Okay, someday I would love to.'

'What does your father do?' Mrs. Sharma intervened.

'He is an editor-in-chief in the Dehradun weekly,' I said turning all my attention to her.

'That's pretty nice. Then you must work in his press. Why take this pain?'

'I don't like taking favour from him. What's the use of education if back up was all I needed?' I said giving a smile to Gautam.

'That's a great thought,' she said and looked at Shreya. We talked for hours and it was late until the time for dinner arrived.

'Okay, enough of this interview. I think we must get eating now.' she said.

We got up from the living room to go to the dining room. It was great watching Gautam assisting his mother while I stood at a distance. Shreya watched television in the dining room and called me back there. I went to join her and sit there while Mrs Sharma laid the table.

I insisted to help her but she refused to take any sort of help from me. Mrs. Sharma said this was a task that she loved to keep to herself.

As I moved in the living room I said to Shreya, ' she sure she's fine? I mean we could help her.'

In the meantime, Mrs. Sharma also came back to the room.

'Yes, it's her favourite task. I feel so relaxed at times for somehow, I repel cooking. She has not let us touch the table since we were kids. And guess what, even when she is not well no one can do the cooking other than her. She won't let either me or Gautam lay the table.' Shreya held Mrs Sharma and said pulling her cheeks. 'Get away you notorious girl.' Mrs Sharma said.

'I know you are a wonderful cook and am dying to have something cooked by you the soonest possible.' Shreya chuckled.

'Well, whenever you want. It's just up to you whenever you wish to come.' I smiled at her.

By now the table was laid and we took the chairs. Mrs Sharma served the dinner to everyone. Her every move was tailored and stitched. I wondered if she had the etiquettes since forever or developed them as a part she grew. The unparalleled ways she had made me think if it was just her or Gautam's father had also imparted a portion of his personality in Gautam. It was too soon to imagine anything so I simply ate and kept my quiet.

The whole evening, we talked and laughed. The meal cooked by Mrs Sharma was delicious. The food was vegetarian, though she had prepared a few non-vegetarian items for me as she took cookery classes while she was in France for a month on assignment during a fashion show. And I was surprised at how adeptly she had prepared it, even without tasting it. After having the meal, we had the dessert together. Everything she prepared was off the charts. I just loved her style of cooking. At around eleven in the night I left from there. Gautam came to drop me home and Shreya also joined us for she had to buy something.

'Visit us again,' Mrs. Sharma hugged me and I finally felt comfortable in her company and realised after all she was just a simple lady. The professional outlook is so different from when you know people personally.

As we drove off we stopped at a cafe to get some coffee. Shreya and I sat in the car while Gautam went to get the coffee. 'You know this is his favourite cafe; we three visit her whenever Ma says. Strangely it happens to be the favourite cafe of all three of us.'

'Are you kidding me, really?'

'Wow then it seems we can hang around here more often.'

'Oh sure.'

Through the freezing weather outside, I saw Danish and Jessica. They were smoking cigarettes. I showed them to Shreya and told her they were my friends. I stepped outside and to meet them. In the meantime, Gautam also returned. As he saw me with Danish, his expression changed.

'Hi Gautam,' Danish greeted him.

'Hi, how do you know my name?'

'Well.' Danish looked at Jessica and shrugged, Jessica looked at me and shrugged and I looked at Gautum. 'Avisha! Really? This is what guys do, tell the entire planet about the girl they love other than her, and guess I'm the girl here.'

All of us laughed.

'Let's get you home. It's late and mother might be worried I have to drop this little girl home,' He said pointing Shreya. Jessica gave me an inquisitive look but I gestured to explain things later to her.

We said bye to them and left. While returning to the car he gave me a parcel.

'I want you to read it when you reach home.'

We bumped in the car and he drove silently to drop me home. When we reached home I hugged him and Shreya and fared them a good night. After they left I opened the letter on the stairs.

'Dear Avisha, I wanted to say this but was too nervous to speak. I've never expressed my feelings to anyone before so I'm at loss of words, what to say. I see you so close to me. At times I was pushed and pulled to go away from you. But, it doesn't happen now anymore. I know you loved someone else but tell me, did you feel complete there? Did you feel what you feel with me? I love you. Even if it doesn't matter in the future or whatever goes around in our lives I wish I knew you much better. More than that I that I wish I had never fallen in love with you. I know it because what I feel for you I will never feel my entire life again for someone else. And if you're gone, maybe, it'll be the end of belief in me. The passion that we grow together is at place clutching my heart. Though, even if I feel I can fade it off and shed you off with a few shrugs I know it won't happen. As the time is passing I am falling in love with you even more. It was supposed to end as they say, when we were at distance but why didn't it happen? You are around in fact you should not be here with me all the time. I feel your presence walking with me. What if you chose to go? Or you chose not to love me anymore. They say one-sided love hurts, when it starts to kill you. You cut me into pieces every day when you're away and I can't stop loving you; I never could. And I would never be able to. All I wish for is that you be happy my love, my protection and my soul is wandering with you. Just call my name when you need me I promise I'll be around. People say they are fools in love but I want to be your fool. I want to be used by you. Not just now, but forever because even if you accept that I love you and use me, all I would feel is a sense of completeness. I am incomplete without you; I've always been. I tried to ignore your presence and keep myself so busy, that your thoughts don't surround me but I realised when you are in love nothing helps. Nothing, you find a connection, somehow or anyhow. It's just my love, a painful hurting love, that misses you each while. Avisha, let go of all. If I am with you I feel the whole world is at halt and this love is the only thing that exists. I heard people saying 'taking the breath away' but realised it only when I looked at your face, only that I can't look at it knowing it could turn out to be a dream. I've held my guard too high for anyone to come across it. But you burnt it into ashes and now all I see is you, standing with these hands folded across your chest. I wish you knew my love for you are never going to die. It's undying and forever. And when I say forever I mean it.'

I sat on the floor, confused. What was going on in his mind? Was I making him insecure?

LEFTOVERS

As soon I entered the office the next day, I went and kept a letter in Gautam's mailbox. I knew it was the first thing he checked when he came to office.

I waited in my cabin for him to arrive. When he walked in, my heart started thumping. He placed his bag on the desk and opened the drawer to check the mails and filled a cup of coffee for him. I was sitting with my back towards him. He opened the letter and started reading it; I could see his reflection through my desktop.

'Dear Gautam, before I can write anything else I want to ask you something? Are you real or a dream? My heart is living this dream with the same fear as you have. You made me fall in an unconditional love. It gives me the feeling that you're real and that you exist with me as my strength and courage. More than about me, it has become about you. I was always trying to discern if my feelings are genuine for you. I never received any other reply than 'yes.' I respect you, I love you. Your passion drove me all till this point that today if you leave me and go I can't live another day. When you walk around in office you make me nervous. Every day, each single time I have seen you around, I found my heart racing. I can barely breathe. My hands turn cold and I fumble for words around you. It always happens when you see me in the eyes. I can never look at you for I am unable to hide my feelings from you and too shy to express the way I feel. You make me want to live with you. When our hands touch, I feel shots of current in my body. Is that love? Gautam, it's true I had been in a relationship and that we belong to the glamour world. People here change partners even before they themselves know it. But I am not the same and I know you know me too long to know what type of person I'm. I know I don't need to say it to you. I am strong, independent and can take care of myself, but deep inside I am the most basic girl that can't go a day without love. My values don't leave me, Gautam, but, you have to seep in my heart even further. You have to pull me out of myself so that my heart is so bare to you that my body is with me but our hearts are one. I don't know if I can put it better into words. I love you. Be with me forever. Use me if you wish but 'never leave me,' I know your soul, I love your heart.'

He read the letter and came to me, 'Wind up your work by afternoon, we're going out.'

'Where?' I wanted to see his reaction after reading the letter but there was no reaction on his face.

'Anywhere, just you and me.'

'Okay.'

He passed me a smile and left.

It was a hot afternoon as we stepped out. After the long hectic work in the first half, Gautam asked me to go out with him. So we decided to buy two cups of hot coffee and just walk on the roads. It was a casual day but I felt ecstatic for no reason. Gautam asked me where I wanted to go.

I gestured him to come closer. He came near me.

'I have never been to discotheque. Will you take me there?'

'Are you sure?'

'Absolutely' and I blinked my eyes out of happiness.

'Okay then we will go there tonight.'

'Tonight...!' I was surprised.

'Yes ma'am, your wish is my command.'

'Oh...' I winked him an eye.

'Why don't you invite your friends?'

'I think they must be busy. But anyways I'll ask them.' I made a chuckling face, and Gautam pulled my cheeks. I smiled like a child.

We kept walking idly on the streets. After a while we sat on the footpath like idiots. The best thing about Gautam was I could be myself in front of him and he loved me anyways. I didn't have to pretend myself perfect all the time.

I was sitting and sipping my coffee while he stood there casting his shadow on mine. 'What are you doing?' I observed him play. 'Blending in you' he looked at me and smiled.

'But I am here, look' I waved my hand teasing him.

'See there is a part of you here' and he moved to his side inviting my shadow. His gesture welcomed the shadow to perform. I was left speechless and my eyes got teary. He came near me. Holding my hands, he bent on the road and said,

'I don't want to lose any part of you. You have been granted to me with great difficulty my cherubim. Nothing can pull you away from me. I will walk with you and your shadow every moment.' He caressed my hair and moved forward and pressed a kiss on my forehead.

Tears fell from my eyes. I knew Gautam was there standing like a pillar, kneeling like a devotee; I pushed him away and hugged him and wept my heart out. He held me and caressed my head. People stared at us as they passed.

I have never realised if anything could be this pure, before meeting him. I always thought I was in love, before but Gautam made me accept that I didn't know the definition of love. Somehow the day passed tediously. I was filled with life nowadays. Gautam dropped me home while we had to get ready for the party. He left and promised to be back in an hour. So, one hour was all at my disposal to get ready.

I put on the best dress I had and was brimming with excitement. Nahel, Jessica and Danish were also coming. Gautam had invited some of his friends. Today we were going to surprise everyone by telling about us. I was very nervous; Gautam was going to be part of my life today an inevitable part. I looked out of the window and felt so relaxed so calm from within. This was an ecstatic feeling nervous and relaxed at the same time.

I was looking pretty. After a long time, I felt a glaze at my face. It had been years since I kept hearing I had lost my charm. After being left all alone in a way I was just dragging my life but now I felt life again inside me, like I was alive again. I knew it was Gautam and his love. While I was lost in the thought the doorbell rang. I ran to open the door.

'Oh my God.' I shouted out of excitement.

'Yes ma'am. Nahel, Jessica, Danish and Gautam flocked in.

'We were supposed to meet at the disc, right?'

'Whatever...' Jessica bumped on the couch. I turned around and looked at Gautam. He shrugged like an innocent child. My most easy victim was Nahel; I went to pull his shirt.

'We will leave. We came to pick you up.'

Gautam said interrupting me. He took me by hands and smiled at me. I smiled at him sceptically.

'Come on', he took me to the door and closed it behind me.

Jessica went to have water. It was just us outside the apartment now. Roses, more roses; Bouquets, more bouquets, the whole fifteen-floor was decorated with them. I got teary. I couldn't utter a word and knelt on the ground. Gautam didn't try to hold me. He was overwhelmed to see me happy. He knelt on the ground beside me. That is when I heard violins playing from behind all in distorted symphony. I turned around to see Jessica, Nahel, and Danish playing it. I could control blushing. As I got up from floor to go and hit them, Gautam held my hands. Before I could say anything anymore, he hugged me. Tears rolled down my eyes. I couldn't relate anything to reality. But now when Gautam held me, it seemed to be the most obvious thing to me in the discretionary world. I was overwhelmed at the thought of loving him. Of belonging to him; I was his asset he was going to be mine. I stood there, he knelt there. The distance between us was our murderer. It felt in this moment I wanted to be with him. Belong to him. He was in a black t-shirt and blue jeans. His eyes were peeping through his spectacles. The sun was casting its rays on him. He shimmered in it. He looked handsome far more in my eyes. How it happens that when you fall in love with someone, no one seems more beautiful than them? And, if this fact was true, I knew I was in love with Gautam.

If I was in love with Gautam, this meant he was the most attractive man on earth. It was a numb moment for me. Gautam got up and took me in his arms. He made me dance again and I could actually dance. I danced to the rhythm.

It was a melody playing in his heart, transforming in me as dance. I danced with grace. Gautam looked me in the eye. I looked him in the eye. The moment ceased to flow. We could not hear or see anything. He took me in his arms and we swayed. I could hear his heartbeat aloud. I recited his heartbeat. It took my name when it pumped. In a jerk I put a hand on his heart. He kept his hand on my heart. I put my other hand behind his waist, and moved closer to him. I rested my head on his chest. It was heaven. People were ascending and descending from the stairs passing here and there staring at us. But did they exist? Nahel, Jessica and Danish left. They knew we were not going to leave. But they knew we were supposed to be left alone. We went in the room.

My heart stopped me not to fall in love with him. I didn't fall in love. I listened to it. But my heart deceived me. It fell in love with Gautam's heart. They both cheated us.

I decided this very moment I was going to marry him. Live with him. Grow old with him. Have kids with him. Gautam brought his lips near my ears and whispered, while we were dancing.

'You dwell in my heart, Avisha, as its indestructible part. How is it possible for me to love you so madly?'

'My pain, my agony walks with me every moment, Gautam. I love this pain. It makes me realize what an asset you are. I want this pain to be my companion forever. I want to live with you forever. I was living a void life. With no one who loves, who cares, whom did I belong to? No one, my life was so alone I was falling down. You came as a ray of hope. I don't know if I deserve you or not, but you gave me the courage to live on. Seeing you, gives me a new feel – unexplainable and indestructible.'

He kissed on my forehead, and I kissed his hands.

'Let's join our friends, they are inside waiting for you.'

When he said our friends I was surprised, he owned people so easily and had so much conviction about his right that no one could deny him. I couldn't deny him.

IN YOUR HERMITAGE

I was in red top and black half jacket; my hair was loosely tied in a ponytail. Gautam was in a black leather jacket, blue jeans and blue sneakers. Nahel was in a blue navy t-shirt and black jeans, while Jessica wore a red dress. Gautam inspired me to dance. I was imitating his footsteps. He was laughing at my dance. But I didn't care, I knew he didn't, howsoever I danced.

Loud music was deafening our ears. We danced like maniacs. I felt free and elevated. I loved the way Gautam moved. Jessica and Nahel tore the floor by their art of dancing. Danish sat by the bar in the meantime. We had turned into fanatics. Gautam swirled me like a top. In the background the lyrics were, ...'sitting here watching other people live, frozen by the fear to fail, cause everyday there is a war to fight and if I win or lose, never mind, as long as you are my shoulder every night, I used to cry against a wall but now I got a shoulder that I can lean on, swear to me you won't be gone, I am ready for the good times....' a song I loved listening to while I was growing up. Its beats made me dig grooves even back then. I could put it on repeat on my iPod and hear it as long as I was awake. I felt the gap bridging between now and my teenage. I felt drawn back to the child within.

Next song started, '...be with you' by Enrique. I pointed a finger at Gautam and sang the song along with and thumped my feet on the floor.

'...I can't go on; I want to be with you...' I went near Gautam's ear and shouted, through all the noise.

He held my fingers and swirled me like a top. The rotation made me fall on his shoulder. He held me and we danced, breaking the floor and screaming.

Jessica came and stole Gautam from me. Gautam winked me an eye. I thought he was the gravest man on the Earth. I was so wrong about him. He fitted in every sphere of life where I placed him. He enjoyed life, like I had never imagined. I and Nahel were dancing together. I swayed my waist and hands and descended on the floor, while Nahel swayed and stood tall. He swayed, reaching for the floor while I swayed and ascended as his complement. Gautam was looking at me, while he danced with Jessica. I was looking back at him. After few moments, we exchanged partners. It was me and Gautam again. I loved the way he made me move.

It was my first time ever I was in discotheque. Gautam took me by hands and threw me on the floor, never letting go of me. He held my waist and we moved in symphony with the music. His eyes were entangled in mine. I held his waist and moved, making him go back. His killing eyes were intoxicating. I felt dizzy in his arms like I was on drugs. He had a part of me beating in him. I felt so attracted towards him. We forgot who was around us. It was hard to resist his tempting smell. I put my hands on his face feeling him. He smiled and glittered through all the light. I wished to leave this place and go somewhere we could leave alone. He came closer and his look lured my eyes, his breath was reaching me. His every glimpse between my eyelids flickering was appeasing me. He was brimming in my soul. I was overflowing in love.

He swirled me on the floor keeping a hand behind his waist. We danced in our own symphony. Gautam took my hands and kissed it. I kissed his hands too. His passion was making me passionate. I turned on my back, and he held me around my waist. He rested his chin on my shoulder and we swayed. I felt protected, belonged and turned again towards him. I gave him a piercing look he knew I was happy and he reciprocated to express his happiness.

Through all the distance his face came closer to my ear.

'I love you' he whispered.

And hurled me like a top. I didn't have alcohol but already felt the hangover. His love was my alcohol. I was addicted to it. With every beat, my steps were transformed more in him. We were two bodies transforming in one with every passing moment.

I felt carefree. Gautam was there to take care of me. Why would I worry? When we were totally wasted, we went to have something to drink. We had mock-tails and Nahel had shots of tequila. We cheered him and Jessica. Gautam and I didn't drink. It was an insanity we suffered from today. After few shots, Nahel pulled me to the floor. We danced for few more moments. But now we were tired.

'You want to leave now?' Gautam asked me.

'I am starving,' I pointed to my stomach.

All of us were starving so we decided to go to Gautam's place. Gautam called his mother on the way.

'I love you mom. I am coming home with Avisha and few friends. We are starving and want to have something delicious from your hands.' And he laughed.

I leaned out of the window. The wind was as rejuvenating as it never was. It was the most liberating day of my entire life. I turned back to see Gautam looking at the road and smiling. I smiled at him. He didn't see me but I could see the satisfaction on his face. I felt proud to have made him happy. It was the greatest achievement I had made in entire life.

Gautam was my life, I was convinced even a bit more every time I saw him. Even when I was away from him, he lived in me more than I actually lived inside me.

We reached Gautam's place in sometime. I ran to hug Mrs. Sharma. She hugged me. I could feel the presence of my mother there. I kissed her on the cheek. She embraced me. Gautam's love was where I belonged. Shreya was my little sister. I had become a part of their family.

'I missed you all,' I said.

'I missed you too.' She caressed my head.

Jessica was already in a hangover. She ran to Mrs. Sharma and hugged her. Nahel also came after her. Gautam was smiling. Mrs. Sharma was overwhelmed to see all of us. Nahel and Jessica had never met her before but it felt as if they knew her for ages. Nahel and Jessica hugged her together.

'I love you aunty,' Nahel said.

'I love you more,' Jessica fought with Nahel.

I and Gautam laughed frantically at them. It was since ages I laughed so heartily. I was coming to life again in his love. I looked at Gautam and he blinked his eyes assuring me. I smiled at him. Then we pulled these idiots away from her somehow. They hugged us then. We took them inside the house. Mrs. Sharma laughed as she came along.

DRY ALBEDO

I had a nightmare and woke up in a shock with my knees folded. It was a strange dream and I could not set my mind straight. I could not recollect what the dream was about, even after trying the hardest. I was drenched in sweat and called Gautam at around 3 a.m. in the night.

'Hello, so late, are you okay?'

'I had a nightmare.'

'Are you okay? Do you want me to come?'

'No just talk to me.'

'Okay, what happened, are you fine?' I could feel his concern building.

'Yes. Just talk to me. Be there. Let me sleep.'

'Okay I am here. You are sure you don't want me to come?'

'Yes' I closed my eyes and tried to sleep.

He was there on phone when I fell asleep. After sometime I heard the doorbell ring. I sluggishly got out of bed. I peeped through the keyhole. It was Gautam.

'I am sorry I was concerned.'

I looked nervously at him settling my clothes. He took me to the bedroom. I hugged him and didn't speak for few minutes. He just let me hold him and be there quietly. He took me in his arms and I fell asleep in his lap. He called Mrs Sharma to tell he had reached safely and that I was fine. I was half asleep but I could hear the conversation. In the morning I woke up in bed. Gautam was sitting next to me and smiling. He made me a cup of tea and I rested my head on his lap.

'Get up madam.'

'No...' I rolled in his lap, letting the edge of my hair, touch the ground.

'I am going then.'

'No... Don't go.' I held his hand.

'Then get up.'

'Let me sleep, please.'

'Okay.' He took my cup of tea and was about to sip.

'Wait, that's mine.'

'Now it's mine. Those kids who sleep late don't get anything.'

'No....' I stretched my hands reaching for the cup of tea. He smiled at me and pulled my cheeks. I was in a white shirt and half pants. He took me in his arms and went to the lobby. He put on some rock music and pulled me outside.

I was half awake and he made me dance. I didn't even brush my teeth and he made me dance. I felt insane. My eyes were yet not properly opened. He was dancing in front of me.

'Gautam...' I stretched his name. I hit him on his back, and he nearly toppled on the floor. 'Avisha...' he said it in the same tone.

'You are bad.'

'Go and brush your teeth. Then this baby will get a delicious breakfast cooked by her very own chef.' And he bowed in style.

I thumped my feet on the floor and went to brush my teeth. I heard him laugh behind me and turned to give him a frowning look. While I returned after brushing, I felt sleepy already. I saw he was in kitchen, so I tried sneaking in the bedroom again to sleep. I was almost halfway in the room when I heard him just behind me,

'Where are you going?' I felt like a culprit.

'Um... to change clothes.' I made an innocent face.

'Oh yeah...?'

'Yes...' I shrugged innocently.

'Yeah...?'

'Yes...' I was embarrassed at being so lazy. He put his arms around me and I smiled. Then he raised me in his arms and took me to lobby. He threw me on the couch and came near me. He put an arm around me and tickled me with the other. I was laughing uncontrollably. I couldn't help it. I tried running away from him but he didn't let me loose. He tickled me for as long I didn't cry.

'Are you still sleepy' he smiled at me.

'No...' I nearly cried.

I supported my face on the table with a hand and looked at him while he fed me. I loved his eyes that had a mystifying attraction. They were looking through his spectacles. His small lips were sealed. He smiled at me as he fed me. I looked at him with eyes full of love. He gave the look like I was a small baby. But I was a grown up. I wanted to be where he was. As he advanced his hand to feed me I held it. I kissed it with the most unintentional intentions. He looked at me and smiled. I got up from place and went ahead to sit in his lap. I arrested him with my hands around his neck. I could see the blush on his face. He leaned to carefully put the plate on the table behind me. His hands were on my waist to keep me from falling. I looked at him and smiled. He brushed my nose with his finger.

'Are you tempting me to marry you? The deal seems fair but, you have to be like this forever.' I whispered to him in a spoilt tone.

'Well after marriage, I have heard men change. They want only one thing from their woman you know.'

'Ok... Let me hear what that is?'

'Really...? You want to know?

'Well in all fairness, I do sir.'

'Be sure, you might have to repent your decision Miss Avisha.'

'Come on, I don't repent my decisions.'

'Are you sure?'

'Of course, yes.' With a jerk he put his hand behind my waist and pulled me close. I was taken aback.

'You still want to know.'

I couldn't reply. I fumbled for words. Gautam looked at me with passion. He moved his face near mine. I tried setting my hands free from his grip but I had no strength. He was smiling mischievously at me. His face came near mine. I closed my eyes for I knew nothing was in my control.

I felt his lips press against my chin and he opened his hands. I jumped from his lap and ran in the bedroom to lock the door from inside. I was breathing heavily. I heard the main door open.

I stepped out the room to see he was gone. I stood there wondering what just happened. I sat on the floor feeling his presence within me; he had become a part of me.

After sometime, I gained some sense and got ready for office. I couldn't concentrate on anything. His smell was all around. I knew he was as embarrassed as I was. Most of the time we were normal but after these moments' things become so uneasy that the situation always went out of our control. We were crazy in his love.

ME AND THEE

Gautam visited my flat along with Shreya. I wasn't a good host but Jessica and Nahel were also there so it gave me some strength. I was smiling at Gautam. He had visited me many times before but it was a formal visit making me nervous. Whenever I looked at him he smiled at me. He knew I didn't want to turn Shreya off and was trying my hardest. They had come for dinner.

Gautam brought some fruits and flowers for me while Shreya prepared a chocolate cake which she brought for me. Jessica hugged Shreya and I could see Nahel had started flirting with her right away. Gautam showed his protective instinct and revolved around Shreya to save her from the ridiculous claws of Nahel. I went to him and assured that it was fine, and Shreya or Nahel were not kids.

At first, he was hesitant but when I emphasized, he was convinced but warned me, to which I smiled and shrugged. Then three of them went to the terrace to see the stars through the new telescope that Nahel had brought. He had developed this latest habit of star gazing and often came late night to see the stars from my terrace along with Danish and Jessica. We talked for entire night while Danish prepared coffee. The telescope lied in a corner after initial five minutes once our conversations caught hustle.

After they left, I and Gautam were left alone in the house. I was cooking in the kitchen. It was the fateful day when I cooked for Gautam for the first time. He was standing beside me making me conscious. I looked at the utensils escaping his eyes. He never visited my house very often and I was not an excellent cook but I wanted him to love whatever I cooked. Not because I wanted him to like it but because I pined for him to love everything about me.

'What are you cooking?' He came beside me and tried to make out what I was cooking.

'Wait and watch for yourself' I said without raising my head and trying to sound as normal as I could.

'Can I taste it?' he asked.

'Not yet.'

'Why?'

'I'm not done' he made me act weird intentionally. I asked him to go out of the kitchen because I wanted to surprise him but he leant on the marble slab and looked at me.

'Go…' I pushed him out.

Instead of going out he pulled me close and I lost all control. My hands started shivering. He took me in his embrace and sniffed at my neck. I was unsure of that moment. I could not meet his eyes. His hands reached for my waist, and I felt a shot of current running through my nerves. He looked me in the eyes and it felt like he was looking at something else. Not me; someone inside me. Like there was someone there he didn't know. His fingers ran through my lips. I looked at him in the eye and tried reading his thoughts. He held me tightly and tears fell down his cheek. I hated to see tears in his eyes but loved when they brimmed in love for me and only me.

'What happened?' I held his face.

'You are going to be my wife.' He whispered.

'I already am; only a ceremony would bind us together and give a name to this relationship. I have accepted you from my heart and soul. I love you, my angel,' I whispered.

That is when we realised the hooligans returning, so, we separated within a fraction of seconds. Gautam wiped his eye and left from the kitchen. Jessica and Nahel helped me in laying the table. They were my only family here other than Gautam's. I care for them like I do for my own family or Gautam's family.

After dinner Nahel played some songs on guitar while we listened to him. Then Shreya sang a song perfect to lift our mood. She was an awesome singer.

With every lyrical note that Nahel described in his song I felt a different sensation. As if I was falling in love for the first time. Gautam was sitting next to Nahel and when I looked at him continuously. He seemed new. He seemed a total stranger to me – a stranger, whom I was deeply attracted to. A stranger who had taken my heart. The feelings were undiscovered and strange like I was reliving the couple of moments that I have lived in my childhood. As the songs went on, on a higher note, there was a quiver in my heart like it was hit by an earthquake. I shivered physically. I had to look around noticing that no one saw me shiver with the surge of emotions. He was near to me and the delicacy was reflecting on his face. He didn't look at me or he didn't want to. He wanted to avoid me and I wanted to look at him. I wanted him to see what my eyes said and read what his eyes spoke. There was an absolute silence other than the song that Nahel sung.

I saw the mirror in my balcony only to find a new person each day. Through the shimmering light of night, his face was glowing as he just washed his face and the water had still not left his skin completely. I was totally absorbed in him. In a moment his face turned to me. I looked away trying to pretend but my face immediately turned at him. He looked at me and I gestured him to learn what was he looking at. He nodded his head to convey that it was nothing. Though I knew what he was looking at and he knew what I was looking at for so long.

When they were done with singing, it felt we came in some other world. Then they had left. Gautam too left with them. He promised to call me as soon as he reached home.

BENEVOLENCE

I was awake and waited for Gautam's call. It was already an hour and he had not yet called. I called him but he didn't pick so I kept trying but there was no answer. I waited for ten minutes but he didn't call back so I called him again. There was no reply. I was bewildered as he had always received my call, howsoever busy he was. I called his landline but no one was there so I left a voice message. My feet were going numb thinking why hadn't he picked up the phone?

'Gautam, please pick up.' I spoke to myself as I dialled his number with my shivering fingers. There was no response so I called Nahel.

'Can you please come here and take me to Gautam's home. He is not taking my call. I am vexed if he is okay.'

'Relax, let me call Kuber and take his number. Don't you have his other number?' That is when I saw Shreya's call waiting on my phone. I told Nahel to receive it.

I tried to speak with a contained tone, 'Are you guys alright and why is Gautam not picking up my call?'

'We met with an accident and he is in ICU.' She sobbed as she spoke.

'What, where are you?'

She gave me the address and I immediately took a taxi and rushed to the hospital pressing my lips tightly as tears fell down. Each minute that passed seemed to take away my breath. As soon as I reached the hospital then I rushed in.

'Madam, your fare...?' The taxi driver shouted from behind.

'Shit I forgot my wallet.' I pressed my head and gave him my gold chain and address and phone number to return it sometime and take the fare.

'I can't take this.'

'See I've no money and I've a dear one admitted in the hospital, please try to understand.'

'Take this chain back, this is my card call me anytime at your place when you need a taxi I'll take the money then.'

I was overwhelmed at his kindness,

'You're an angel.' I said and left.

Shreya was at the reception waiting for a doctor.

'Where is he? Is he okay?' I clutched her shoulder, 'Are you okay?'

'He hurt his head severely and the doctor suspects he might have had a brain haemorrhage.'

'How did it happen?'

'A drunk truck driver hit us from behind and in trying to save a two-wheeler with two kids, we fell in the valley. Though it wasn't deep enough, he has been severely hurt. Luckily, I opened the door and fell on the road. I got no other scars than few scratches on the arms and elbow.'

'Can I see him?'

I took deep sighs and held Shreya. Somehow, I felt Gautam's presence within me. I kissed Shreya on forehead and told her not to worry. I went to Mrs. Sharma who was trying to be strong but when I held her she broke down.

'Don't worry he'll be fine. I have seen even worse cases of haemorrhage where people easily recover.'

'I wish so. But has the doctor confirmed that it's a haemorrhage?'

'I don't know. I just heard Shreya saying'

'Then please don't say that. I'm already so worried.'

'Me too.'

A doctor came out of ICU and looked at Mrs. Sharma.

'His condition is very critical. I can't say if we will be able to save him. Pray to God.'

His words had an immediate emotional and physical effect on us as he walked down the corridor. Mrs. Sharma fainted on ground and I felt the whole hospital revolve in front of my eyes. I sprinkled few drops of water on her face and she came back to senses but very feebly. No one talked anything to anyone as we sat there. His face was coming in front of my eyes again and again. My heart was aching as someone was cutting it into pieces. I rarely felt at such a loss in my life. God had gifted me the most precious gift and was taking it away. The nurses were passing in front. Shreya went to every other nurse that came asking about Gautam. I had to console her, make her sit down. The doctors had kept him under observation for three days.

We sat there the entire night. In morning I sent Mrs. Sharma and Shreya to home. They were adamant to go at first. But I convinced them to take rest so that they could be there for the next day. It was eleven in the morning of next day and I was standing in front of the ICU. The door opened and a nurse stepped out of. Gautam was visible from within. There was a drip on his left hand. His head was plastered and face swollen. My eyes gaped as I couldn't believe what they saw. His entire face was bruised and as the door closed behind the nurse I stared at the closed door. Gautam was lying so distant to me. I fell on the ground and didn't know whether to believe my eyes or not. I didn't know if it was all real. Gautam promised that he won't ever leave me but I wondered if he could keep his promise.

I was pacifying my mind and pressing my heart firmly to stop crying but I failed every time. When I could no longer control myself, I ran to the washroom and screeched out of pain. I pulled my hair and shouted. I shouted as my whole world was ending in front of me and I couldn't do anything. I was trying to be strong but could no longer hold on to my guts. How could I? What was I without him? I had no existence if he wasn't there. He made me alive. If he left me I couldn't help but go after him, wherever he would go.

'Gautam, come back. I love you. You can't leave me. You are there right? You are listening right? Tell me...answer Gautam. You are there...? You can hear me Gautam...' a nurse came and asked me to pull myself together.

Why couldn't I make myself strong? I had to take care of Mrs. Sharma and Shreya, but I couldn't.

God had played with the beauty of Gautam. When I blinked my eyes his smiling face came in front. I couldn't shut my eyes and was terrified to see the apparition of his smiling face in front of my eyes. I compared his smile to his face now. I would have been more delighted to bear all his pain if I could because I couldn't see him in pain. I was the one who should have been at his place. I shouted at God and accused him of being so unreasonable. He couldn't play with his life, right?

Gautam didn't deserve to be sleeping on the bed senselessly, instead I was supposed to take away all his pain, to protect him and take all his troubles on me. I was there to veil him in my protection. I felt disgusted at my presence; here I was breathing so shamefully and Gautam's breath had to be regularized.

I looked at the mirror, 'It's all because of you. You are the murderer.

You are born to destroy everyone's life. If he didn't come to your home he would have been fine by now. How can you be so selfish?' I was too disgusted to even look at my face.

He met that fate just because of me. I punched on the mirror and it broke into pieces. Blood started flowing from my hands but I couldn't feel any pain. My tears did not stop as the blood drained through the sink. I put my hand under the tap frantically not letting the blood stop. I wanted to die then and there.

I realized someone pulling me from there. It was a nurse. She pulled me out of the washroom and shouted at me. I couldn't hear her. My eyes were looking at the floor and cried. That is when I realised someone holding me. I raised my eyes to see Nahel.

He was crying. I never saw him cry before. I hugged him.

'Please save him Nahel. Please do something.'

'He will be fine. Don't worry he will be okay.' He held me.

I didn't realise when I got dizzy and fainted in his arms.

WOODEN HEART

When my eyes opened I saw a bandage on my hand. I was lying on a bed in the hospital and when I got up, it took me moments to realise why I was here. I ran out of the room to reach for him. I saw Nahel roaming in the lobby and went to him,
'How is he now and what did the doctors say?'

He turned to me in bewilderment, 'his condition has worsened. Doctor has said there is only one percent chance that he will be able to recover.' His voice was very low like he said from stomach and put all his effort to make it audible. He couldn't raise his head and meet my eyes as tears were swelling over the brim of his lower eye-lid.

'Don't say this, please tell me you are lying.' I scratched his hand with my nails as I nearly toppled on the ground petrified by the news. He looked away and tried controlling his tears.

'You are lying right? He is alright I know. Why are you lying?' I looked at his face, expecting him to laugh and tell me, Gautam is okay now. But his expressions didn't change. He didn't raise his head.

I held his arms. All my strength diffused into the air. I was shivering and fell on the ground.

'Tell me what should I do, I will do anything?' Nahel pulled me from the ground and put his arms around me, 'Avisha, be strong. Pray to God; let your love be there for him. There is nothing more you can do for him at this point of time.'

'He won't go anywhere. I won't let him go anywhere, and who is God to decide whether I deserve him or not; enough of His games. I love him and it won't set him free.'

I saw Gautam walking through Nahel's shoulder.

'Gautam...' I got up. Nahel turned around.

'There is no one there.' He said and held me.

'See he is there' I shouted '...Nahel look he is there.' My eyes swayed between Gautam and Nahel.

Nahel held me and put my head on his shoulders. I looked again and there was no one there. Gautam was gone.

'You made him go away. Why didn't you let me go to him...?' I shouted like a maniac. Nahel slapped me hard on the face.

'Come to your senses, Avisha, there is nobody there.'

I looked at Nahel and silently, I cried.

We got up and he took me to the doctor.

'When can we see him?' I asked. 'You can go but make sure you make no noise.'

I was standing outside the ICU. Gautam was lying inside. My hands were trembling as I was dying to see how he was. I entered the ICU taking out my slippers. It was dim in there and he was lying unconscious there. My heart was at peace, just being around him.

I felt as his bride; like he was looking at me. I could see his eyes, beyond his eyelids. I went over to him. Even in this condition he was handsome. The drip was falling drop by drop. A pipe entered his nose. His lips were dry and mouth opened. I sat on the stool beside him. He was there and looked like an angel; I knew I was in love with that angel.

'Gautam, you know you stole my heart the first time I saw you. I was so confused if I loved you. But Gautam, I love no one else, only you. You are meant to be in this heart forever. I looked at you through those distances, and loved you every while.'

I took his hands in mine. His grip tightened. He was unconscious, but his grip tightened. I smiled at him. I stood and went over to his face. My hand caressed his face.

'Angel...' I said with sore throat. I looked at him, capturing his face for entire life. My fingers touched his lips, and went to his forehead, then his mischievous eyes, then his gleaming nose. I looked at his lips, stared at it.

'Gautam...' I said.

I caressed his forehead, 'You know how beautiful you are. You will never know it angel. You don't know what you are. Only I know it. No one knows who you are. I am blessed to have you. Even if I want I can't explain. No language can put it in words, what creation of God you are! Your gesture drives me mad, veiled in your heart. These arms shine through miles, tempting me.' and a smile spurted from my lips.

I saw his lips tremble. His eyes flicker. I don't know if it was my imagination but I saw it. I had faith; nothing was going to happen to him. He belonged here. He belonged with me. I was convinced his pain was a test we had to pass together.

Suddenly the doctor came inside and asked me to leave. I didn't say any other word and came out. I knew he was going to be okay. Lost in my thoughts, I went over to Mrs. Sharma. Something was bewildering me badly. I wanted to say something. I knew it was killing me. But what it was, I didn't know. Something was tending me ambiguous. So, I went to Mrs. Sharma

'Can I ask your permission for something?' I looked at her with eyes full of hope.

'Yes...' she said in broken words, confused at my accent.

'Can I marry your son?' I asked and then I realised that was what I wanted to speak.

'This is what I wanted.' I felt at ease after deciphering my thought in words. She looked at me in surprise.

'Yes' and hugged me.

I couldn't understand her gesture. For a moment, I felt lost in her arms. On realising the whole scenario, I was too overwhelmed to say anything further. Pulling myself together I put my head in her lap,

'I want to be a part of your family. I don't want to be acquainted to you anymore. I want to be related to you now. I want you to be my mother. I want Shreya to my sister. I want Gautam to be my husband. Is it possible for you? Is it possible for you to love me like you love Gautam?' tears rolled down from my cheek on her sari, and she caressed my head and wiped my tears.

'Yes, I accepted you as my daughter the first time Gautam brought you home. And you didn't prove me wrong Avisha. The way you have stood here with us, depicts how largely you understand the meaning of the term 'family.''

My heart got heavy with her affection and love. I broke down and sobbed like a child. She hugged me and both of us cried. No one said anything beyond this. Only silent tears marked our stories with every drop shed. We didn't speak but both of us knew, we were missing Gautam at that moment.

PERPLEX

I was sitting in the hospital canteen, having tea and biscuits with Mrs. Sharma. She was in a light yellow sari. Her forehead had a black bindi. She was telling me the stories of Gautam's childhood. How he grew up, what he liked or disliked. At times she cried and had to wipe off the tears with the corner of her sari. From a distance I saw Nahel coming, as he reached us he greeted Mrs. Sharma and looked at me,

'When did you come?' I was surprised to see him.

'Just now. I went inside to see you when Shreya told me you are at the canteen. It's a miracle. You know Gautam has showed some improvement today, he opened his eyes. Doctor was saying one in thousand cases show such rapid recovery.' Nahel said while I was sipping tea, he was almost panting.

My face gleamed, 'Really? Is there any possibility I could see him?'

'No baby, not so easily. Where is my reward for bringing the good news?' I hit his face, and ran for Gautam, and Nahel followed behind, he winked at Mrs. Sharma.

I was sure Gautam would recover. I had all my faith in him.

I was elevated, as I reached the ICU; I smiled at the door, as I could see him, as he reciprocated my smile like he always did. I was walking in front of the ICU briskly. I couldn't control myself from going in. I waited for some doctor to pass from there eagerly.

Soon, a nurse passes, I held her hands, 'Can I please go inside for two minutes?'

'No, miss it's not the right time.'

'Please, let me in for only two minutes.'

'No, it's against the hospital rules.' It was then I saw Nahel showing her a hundred rupee note trying to bribe her, and to my surprise, her expressions changed. I looked at him, and looked back at the nurse who was at first hesitant. 'Please be back in five minutes.' She whispered softly taking the note from his hands.

I shook my head smiling and reaching for Gautam. He rested peacefully on his bed there, like he was waiting for me. Tears started rolling down my eyes; I walked softly and reached him, and held his hand. I saw him smile a bit; I held his hands and kissed it. I put his hands on my face and cried. He smiled slightly at me.

'I love you.' I said. He tried saying something, but his strength was failing him, so I put my hands on his lips, and smiled at him,

'I know you love me too.' I could feel his lips smile under my palms, so I smiled again.

'Get well soon, we have to make so many preparations for the marriage, can you believe I asked your mother about the marriage and she had the similar plans in her mind for us. It's so insane; I should've been the boy...' I was chirping stupidly to him, first time I didn't feel conscious in front of him. It was all too good to be true. Maybe it was all because he didn't speak. When I used to hear his voice, I was always left speechless. I could close my eyes and identify him from his voice across miles. Gautam was smiling slightly; his eyes had the same attraction as ever.

I looked at him and wondered if it was true. My heart was aching badly with joy, I thought I didn't deserve his love. Not only did I think, but also, I was sure about it. I was the culprit who deserved to die. And here I got Gautam in my life, which not only made me love him, but also, taught me the meaning of belongingness. Life without him was now impossible for me. I couldn't stay another moment denied of his presence, in my soul. His eyes were gleaming, I held his hands, and put it on my heart. I could see the goose bumps on his hands. He could not speak but his hands were saying it all. I saw his eyes getting red, and tears started falling down from the corner of his eyes. I stared at him for a while, and then went ahead to wipe his tears. I took his hands to my cheek and kissed them. Then I moved towards him, and gave him a bit of support. I lied in the little space next to him. He was still crying and tears were falling down his eyes. I kissed him on the eyes, and held him.

'I am here, don't worry. I am here forever. Not to go anywhere. Not to leave, but to love you and only you as long I am here Gautam. Here on this earth.' His tears were dropping on my hands, and I couldn't bear his silence. Why didn't he speak? I was missing his voice. I closed my eyes and supported my forehead on his nose. He put a bit of pressure and his hands tightened on my face.

'Never leave me.' his voice came out in a vague whisper. I was trying to hold back my tears till then, but after hearing his voice, there was a shiver up my spines. I could not help myself. I broke down in his bosom, his chest. I grabbed him tightly and cried. He tried to caress my head with his other hands and I could feel his fingers moving slightly in my hair, making me cry even harder. 'Gautam, how did I get you? I don't deserve you. I don't. I don't at all. I had been holding back my tears for so long. I was like a dead body that could feel the pain, but couldn't respond to it. You have given me smiles my angel, but more so ever, returned to me the sensation to feel. I can cry now. I can feel now. I can love now, again. If someone ever asked me if angels existed, I would always point you out because you are my angel. You are the God I have ever seen, and believed to exist.'

VELVET

Gautam was leaning on the railing of his balcony. He held a coffee mug, in a light green short kurta and peach pyjama. His left hand was still bandaged. I stood about a metre from him. My eyes looked keenly at him as he was drinking coffee. Though I knew, he wanted to say something, but, at the same time, I found him struggling. His eyes had the same uneasy stare that always shook me. Other than that, he gave a serious look to the coffee mug. I wished to ask him what bewildered him, but rather stayed quiet giving him time to figure out his words. I moved inside the room and sat on the bed, at a distance from him, to make him more comfortable.

'Avisha' he whispered in the lowest mumble when I had hardly set my foot on the floor of bed.

'Yes' I replied in a similar tone, figuring out what he had to say, avoiding his eyes at the same time, making gestures that I was not nervous. Though I was dying to hear what he had to say, at the same time I wished he stayed quiet and said nothing. His voice made me too vulnerable.

He looked at me and I couldn't wait any longer to listen to his words. He kept the mug aside, leaned on the railing, looked outside and then looked at me again.

'Why did you come in my life?'

'What do you mean?'

'I...I...' before he could say anything further I found myself clutching the corner of the bed. His voice was too heavy to handle. It was difficult to handle his silence, or his words. His voice pierced my heart. I felt the tides surging in my veins, and his eyes were passionate enough to let me be moulded in his words any moment he wanted. My heart pained.

He folded his arms rigidly across his chest. I didn't look at him, for I failed in courage to look at him now. I knew he felt something strongly, that he died to say. I wanted to be able to help him out. But it was strange that as long he didn't say anything, I was at peace, as if his words took the heart out of me.

'I... found...you....' and he paused again struggling for words'...you protected my family, while I expected none of this from you. I never thought anyone would be there for my family as much as I was.' He paused again,

'Please tell me, Avisha...' his voice was like an arrow…. why, why are you so there with me every moment. I live my life, but I always feel your presence around. Like you're watching me or walking with me. The height of my madness has taken me to a level where I even customise my actions in order to please you, or seek your attention, when the fact is you're not around.' and he opened his folded arms and broke down, cupping his face.

He fell on to the ground on his knees.

I was shocked to see him. I didn't know what sensation I had, I couldn't see him cry. Nearly tumbling on floor I ran and knelt in front of him. I took his hand in mine.

'Are you mad, Gautam? How could you say it? Do you even know how you made me alive? I was dead Gautam, you know I was...' and before I could say anything further, he pulled me tightly in his embrace.

'You know, Avisha; I don't know how I found you.'

I was left speechless. His embrace was too powerful for me to escape and to weave my thoughts in words.

'I love you Gautam.' I put his hand on my heart, parting from him, looking him in the eye.

He ignored my gesture and smiled.

'Never leave me. I don't know what I could do without you. I was a dead body; you have filled me with life. I could meet such thousand accidents to feel your care. It makes me alive till my endless nerve, my Angel.' he kissed my nose. 'I could be betrayed, hurt, decomposed thousand times to be moulded in your piece of art. I love the way you possess me. The way...' he put his hands on my mouth, and I shivered.

'Don't speak, just don't speak.' he embraced me delicately, in a tender moment.

But, I always wanted him to hold me in a similar way so that I could not breathe. And there, he was holding me to make me his, forever.

'Gautam, we both know we love each other. Then why this distance between us? Why we become so conscious in each other's presence? Is it right?' my voice softened and I said in a delicate tone,

'Your love has taken me in some other world.'

He smiled, and I smiled back at him. He lifted me up in his arms, and carried me to his room. He opened a closet. I was too puzzled to say anything to him. I looked at his shining eyes that were clueless and staring at the grey cupboard. Not many days back, I was blaming God for treating me the way he did. I blamed God for not loving me enough. And he sent me to Gautam, to make me explore the meaning of life in true sense. I knew the purity of Gautam was so real, so beautiful that I couldn't escape the grip of it. He had the tender heart of a kid, and it was showed every time when he laughed. He took out a photograph and gave it to me.

There were four people in it. Gautam, Mr Sharma, Shreya and his father. 'Avisha, after all that he did to us, I don't know why I still miss him at times.' Gautam looked at me like a culprit.

'It's your heart that still loves him. You can't see the evil in evil and look with optimism everywhere.' I looked at him.

'I wish to see him now. At least ask him once, what went wrong. Why he left us alone? What was so important to him that we didn't matter a bit.' He shook his head in disappointment.

'Things will be perfect. I promise. You are the best person I've known and I am absolutely sure that nothing can ever go too wrong with you. Things are destined to sort themselves out, and they will do. Whether you want it or not. Just wait for the right time. For the person you are, life is going to be beautiful. Trust me.'

I assured holding his hands.

'I don't know how unnoticeable I or my family could be for him. How did he just not see us? Yes, I know I am alive, and I live each while to discover myself, which I don't know yet. But every day the harder I try the more I lose myself. Before you came in my life I was fighting to get a grip. It's so difficult holding on when you are losing yourself. I got it through you. It's awful but life felt so empty, that I wanted to finish it forever and trust me, the way my family smiles from the surface it's just for display. You'd never guess or see the kind of pain we go through each while. It's tough, so tough to fight, but I've to forsake of my family. And though unbearable, and the harder I try to keep them safe and protected, the closer I'm drawn to them. It's tough for my mother to know each while; there is no one she counts on for her life, other than us. I can't explain that what you've done for me. Even when I was lying there in the ICU my mind was occupied by the thought how they will be coping up. But every time I saw you, each time you visited I was assured that I was there with them. Trust me, you are me, and I'm you. We are not two different people but the same.' and he held my hands.

'I know it's difficult for you to understand what I went through and maybe you won't but it's easy for you to be around me, and that you do which is the biggest thing in itself.' he drew the statement by putting both my hands on his heart.

'It's not about understanding. It doesn't matter if I understand you or don't. It's about feeling you. Feeling what you feel, going through what you do and still holding on and never letting go of you. This I've learnt that life is not about being compatible, it's about belonging. As long you belong somewhere you are alive. There is a shelter you can go back to. There is a sense of feeling that yes you are taken care of, I want to give that to you, and need the same from you. It's not about what I regret or forget. It's about being alive to the realities and holding on to the truth, despite the dense fog of lies. As long as we are holding on to each other everything is pure. Don't worry about anything. Nothing is going to pull you down. The kind of faith and trust you've planted in me has made me alive and it makes me feel I've gained the purity that my soul had lost. I love you. As purely your heart beats, it mingles with mine even if you don't say it, even if I don't see it. Do you feel it? Do you feel our love? I know you suffered but, let your father have a chance. Maybe he fell in love. Or say, maybe he wanted to comeback. How do you know what's true unless you've seen it?

If you felt it from the core that he didn't care maybe you're right. But, there will be so many people who'll love you and just be there for you, for the wonderful person you are. Just don't let that fall.'

I slowly put my head on his bosom.

'You know when I first saw you; I knew you were like me.'

'I did notice you every moment, since I first saw you. You were never far from me, never. You have transformed me to someone else, someone yours. All I pray to God is you. If I have you, I've everything.'

I said only the truth for true love is the only essence that establishes you, and you turn to in times good or bad.

He smiled and put his arms around me tenderly.

This is when Shreya and Mrs. Sharma entered the room. They had just returned from the market. We parted, and he went away while I wiped my eyes and put on a smile on my lips.

'Is everything okay?' Mrs. Sharma asked.

'Yes' I tried changing the topic.

She moved forward and pressed a kiss on my forehead.

GRAPHITE

We walked with slow steps in the lawn in the morning. The doctor had asked him to walk in fresh air. Mrs. Sharma was sitting beside reading newspaper and sipping her hot tea. I lived in Dehradun all by myself, so I came early to his home. I wanted to be around him, I missed him when he was in hospital. To Mrs. Sharma and Shreya, it appeared as I was there to take care of him. But what they didn't know was, I was there just to be around him, every other thing was secondary. It was a pleasant day. Sun was mildly lit, covered by the clouds, still trying to come out. His fragrant smell was travelling with the wind to me. My face was lit up. I was brought to life after so many days. Now that I knew, he was okay and was home talking to me. It was strange how the silence between us was so cosy, so comfortable that when we said it seemed to break the comfort. He at times talked about the weather or passed some remark on the political condition of the city. I nodded my head in approval to whatever he said. Sometimes while walking, he looked at Mrs. Sharma, who was so busy reading the newspaper that she couldn't realise that he was looking at her. His eyes had a sense of satisfaction that he was on his way to recovery and he was around his family. He pointed her to me and smiled. I returned the smile.

'You know why I didn't die?' while smiling he questioned me.

'Why?' I was taken aback by his strange question but as Mrs. Sharma was around I couldn't say anything.

'To make me understand the value of life. To make me feel this, that I am the luckiest person on earth, with so many beautiful ladies in my life.' He pointed to Mrs. Sharma, Shreya and me.

It was around ten minutes we were walking while the bell rang. Usually he opened the door, so he instinctively moved forward. But Shreya stopped him and went to attend the door. When Shreya returned there was a perplexed look on her face.

'Who was that?'

Mrs. Sharma asked her. Shreya didn't speak anything. Her face had an expression I had never seen before. She forwarded her an envelope. Mrs Sharma saw it and her hands were about to tear it. Gautam moved forward and snatched it from her hands. I could see a disgustful expression appear on his face. He opened the letter as he would tear it. As he read the letter further his expressions became even more distasteful. A mixture of anger and bitterness rested on his face.

'He is not well and wants to see all of us.' He summarised the three-page long letter in just one line.

'He is already dead to us.'

It was Gautam's step mother's letter. Mrs Sharma was so busy reading the newspaper as she didn't listen to a word. Gautam looked to Shreya in approval.

'...But, he is not well. I think you must go to see him at least once.'

I tried to convince him, to at least talk to him once about his health.

'Avisha, shut up. You don't know anything.'

Gautam shouted at me. I was taken aback.

'You don't know what we have faced. You don't know how we lived, unsheltered. What days my mother has seen. He is just another person to me. Just like a stranger I cross paths with in the street. You have no right to interfere in this business. He is not my father. I have no father. My mother is both my father and mother. He is dead to me, he doesn't exist. Do you understand? Just stay out of it. Okay?'

He trembled with nearly tears in his eyes. I knew how embarrassed he was at not being able to hide his tears in front of his family. He never showed them in front of Mrs. Sharma. He had to pretend that he was strong, the strongest man on earth. On the contrary, he was too weak to face these feelings.

'But Gautam...' I tried to speak, but he gestured me to be quiet.

I didn't say a word further for I knew; he had not recovered finally yet.

Shreya who was standing at a distance started crying. I didn't know what to say or what to do. I went ahead and held her. I had never seen Gautam so stern, so unreceptive. I was terrified the way he said.

He left from there, without saying anything.

'Gautam!',

Mrs Sharma called him from behind. He stopped at his position without turning around. I couldn't hold back my tears.

'Go and see him by tomorrow's flight' she said still looking in the newspaper.

'But ma...' Gautam turned around shocked and tried speaking.

There were tears on his cheek. I didn't like whatever went around there and wished I could anything to change his mind. I knew, he wasn't going to listen to me then. There was a deep scar in his heart that had moulded him entirely into someone else. He was tender from within but the shield that he put on himself made it impossible for anyone to penetrate.

'Do as I said,' Mrs. Sharma said once again, making it clear that she wants Gautam to visit his father.

She looked from the gap above her spectacles, bending her head low. That was her way of communicating, that it was her final decision. No one could change her mind, after she had shown that gesture. He looked at me with helplessness. I felt helpless as well. I knew Mrs Sharma could look beyond the whole scene, and was acting in the way; anyone not in the situation would act. She rationalised the whole situation, or maybe, it was her heart that wanted it. It was difficult to tell at that point. However, he didn't wish to go see his father at any cost. When in anger, he saw nothing, not anything at all. He did not shout or speak a word. As long as his thinking was veiled by his anger, he could rarely see outside of it. A leaf that blew in the air, can find no peace, no halt unless the wind stops blowing. Gautam was too simple. He loved people just for sake of loving them and hated only if he had a reason, or, if he had been hurt deeply. His father had not hurt him, but he bruised his life. Gautam could not come into terms with relating his life to that of his father's until then. He was not wrong. It was difficult for a child who waited every day for his father to return, to accept it one day that it was a lie. That the father he waited for so long didn't care about.

And one day, after years, he suddenly realised that he needed to see his family. He returned without tint of guilt. I could sense all that was going within Gautam in one look that he gave me. It was getting difficult for me to handle the environment and Gautam's indifference, so, I went to Mrs. Sharma and told her that I'll see her later.

I left from there. No one asked me anything, I didn't say anything either. All of a sudden I felt like a stranger there. I felt humiliated, I stayed there for him, his love, but if he didn't consider me his own, why had he let me come so close? Why had he let me fall in love with him? I was convinced then, love was just a word. I felt broken; Gautam broke me the worst of all, for I believed he was there only one to mend me. I was untouched by him, but he had already murdered my soul that day. I was not there just to be a part of his happiness. I wanted to accompany him in all walks of life. More than then, I wanted to accompany him to Australia the next day, for he had not recovered. But, I was sure he won't let me come. Maybe, I was over analysing the situation, but I couldn't accept him talking to me so distantly.

ELEGANCE

She was an Australian lady with all the elegant etiquettes that Gautam found in her mother. He wanted to hate her but despite all the efforts, he couldn't.

There was something motherly about her, in spite of the elegance she had. The home was beautifully decorated. Gautam wanted to resist the feeling, but felt strongly at home here. He felt no different than he was at his own home.

As he entered the bedroom, he saw a photograph of Gautam, Shreya and his mother enlarged and framed, on the wall. Gautam's father was lying on the bed. He had wrinkles all over his face and seemed weak because of aging. Gautam wanted to hate him, so much. But he couldn't hate him either. Gautam was standing in front of his father. Gautam looked at him with a strange heart. He had never seen his father in his adolescence. All the pictures that he had of his father were of his childhood. 'Mahesh, Gautam has come' his step-mother woke his father, softly pressing his shoulder. Gautam could not recognise him. The last memory he had of his father was when he was young and handsome.

Looking at his condition then, Gautam's heart skipped a thousand beats. As his father opened eyes, his hands approached Gautam. Gautam held them out of reflex.

'Son, you are handsome. Just like I was in my youth,' he said in soft whisper. Gautam looked in his eyes and he could feel instantly connected to him. The way his mind was conditioned, he was expected to hate him. But how he could hate this frail person. He was too weak even to be hated by anyone.

'I'm not like you sir, I can never be,' Gautam said with disgust, pulling his hand back without looking at him.

'I know you are angry with me and I've no excuse to give you. I'm not worth being forgiven, but I want to confess something, to you.

Will you listen to it?' he said in a crisp weak voice.

'Do I have an option?' Gautam shrugged.

'When you were young, a kid, I was a successful fashion designer. I loved my job and was overwhelmed with the kind of work I did. One day when I was having lunch with one of my friends, I saw your mother for the first time. She was innocent, simple and wore tomboyish attire. I instantly knew there was something special about her. So I asked my assistant to get knowledge of her whereabouts. I approached her for modelling. At first, she was hesitant but later when I insisted, and took her in confidence she agreed. I trained her. She was like my diamond, from the first day I saw her, I bonded with her as I knew her from ages. There was no veil between me and her; we could peep in each other's soul from all the distance. I knew I carved this diamond for the best. She was not difficult to refine, and fashion was in her blood. I fell in love with each of her gestures. She had something so gaudy and grounded that I knew I couldn't be without her for another moment in my life. So, one day I proposed her over coffee. Crazy as she was, she got a ring out of purse and bent on her knees and did what I was supposed to. The whole cafe was for cheering her. I was both embarrassed and ecstatic at the same time. I said 'yes' and son, we were engaged that same moment. We exchanged ring and surrendered our lives to each other that moment forever' his father paused and smiled, and tears rolled from corners of his eyes. He continued, 'We got married and lived happily. But the truth of this glamour world is none lasts forever, so it happened with me. My fame was dawning, and your mother's rising. She was getting lot more recognition that I ever had. I knew she deserved it, I was happy for her. But, then one day another designer asked to sign her for his show. I wanted to let her go, and fly in her career, only because she deserved it. But when she went, I could feel a sense of loss. She would stay out for long hours. I couldn't concentrate on work, and missed her. I worked harder, to avoid her thoughts from creeping in. I retained my position back, more than it was before. I won awards, which I had never won in my previous careers, but I missed your mother. Even for a second that she was away. I loved her too much to let go of her for a moment. I knew she was happy, and she could see I was not. I was successful but not happy. I hated how she read everything that went on within me. All she wanted was to be with me. All I wanted was to be with her. She realised how deeply I missed her when she was away, and she also knew I trusted her blindly. She started making excuses for not going on work, avoiding work. I felt at a loss, for I knew it was me who was binding her. I was bewildered for I couldn't express to her how much I loved her. I didn't want, for any reason she should lose her lustre. She was not my pet, to listen to my orders. I wanted her to soar high, and live her life the way she wanted. And son, my heart and head were rebelling in the most undisciplined way. I knew my love was her only strength, and the more I wanted to give her freedom, the more I couldn't express myself. When I was tired of the tumult, I turned to drugs. She didn't know I was doing drugs. She told me that I was her love, and it was just me that she loved. But, how could I let a lady like her not live her life, and sacrifice it just for me. I knew I had to separate my professional and personal life. I tried letting go of my insecurities, and she helped me with it. But, nothing was helping. So one day I realised, I needed to put an end to it. To leave her there and to let her live her life peacefully without my shadow. Gautam, I didn't marry. Your mother is still my first and last love. The lady you saw is a friend. I didn't want to tell this to you. After I left one day I realised how stupid I was to let go of that lady and make her suffer all this. I wanted to come back to her. But, I thought it was too late. I didn't have answers to the questions you all would've had for me. I loved you all too much to let my insecure shadow to be casted on you all.'

Gautam took a deep sigh, and pushed back the chair. He got up and moved near the window. There was a fountain surrounded by rose bushes, he looked at it and smiled. Then he turned to his father, and smiled again.

'How do you do it? How does mom do it? This much love sacrifice and devotion. She cried each day, Papa' and then he stopped and smiled, 'I wanted to call you 'Papa' since you left. I missed uttering this word, addressing you like this in person. But with time as I started growing, I realised, you weren't the person who deserved it. But now that I know you deserve it. You deserve more than I can say. Why it is so difficult to convey your love to a person whom you love more than yourself, or more than anyone else in the world, even if you know they are yours' I know it very well, and now I know why I can't tell her with ease what she means to me. How at loss of words I am when she is around. It's you Papa; it's your son here.'

'You're in love!' Mr. Sharma exclaimed.

Gautam ignored his statement, 'Ma misses you each while. She never takes your name, never talks about you. But I can see the emptiness in her eyes every day, when she misses you. I always wondered how she could love a person like you. She loves you. She forever has. She forever will. So, you're coming back with me?'

There was a silence.

'I never understood why my heart is so rebellion to every verdict that I had for myself. Why it feels at times to cut and throw it out. Now I know why. Because love is beautiful. As long I knew the poignant origin of it I hated my heart. But now I know how beautiful this small piece of flesh is. It gave me the sensitivity I needed. It gave me the courage to protect Ma and Shreya. It gave me the power to come here and face you. My heart that I hated for falling in love now understands the pure bliss it has given me. I know I can never spare the fact that you left mother for so long. I have seen what she did to get over the pain, and still sometimes I find her sobbing in corners. In front of us, there is always the widest smile on her face, and I know she is happy. She I blessed to have us, me and Shreya. Though howsoever, I might try to hate the fact that we could not be sufficient for her ever. I love her for loving you so much. This is her love that is flowing in my blood, this is your devotion that is flowing in my blood and even though I try to get over it, I know I won't. Never willingly from now onwards. I love whatever God had shown me. I feel blessed to see all this with my living eyes. So much love. Enough of your void in our lives and I can't pretend anymore that we don't need you. We always did and we always will. You have to wait here, till we get it right. Wait here in our lives, not in Australia anymore. We are leaving by tonight's flight,' Gautam said.

Before Mr. Sharma could say anything, Gautam left for getting the tickets done.

Mr. Sharma's hands turned cold, and his lips started trembling. His son was carrying him to the lady of her dreams. They were going to be united, all the days she had spent waiting for him, and she was going to find her love back. They were going to be one again.

'I am overwhelmed by how you've raised our children. I am mesmerised that even in my absence Gautam has turned to be this wonderful human being that I always expected him to be. Thanks for filling our love in them.

Thanks for reminding me again and again why I fell in love with you. I am sorry, but I can never be enough sorry for leaving you there devastated, but I could never love you enough either,' Mr. Sharma whispered.

AURA

For the past half-an-hour Gautam's number was displaying on my phone. Though I pined to pick up the call, something held me back. Maybe it was his indifference, or the way he tried to push me behind, the last time we met. I knew my boundaries and wanted to break them, but his face and his words weren't letting me go. I was too scared to hear what he had to say. What if he never wanted to see me again, what if it was over? Ending a relationship hurt; True, but the sense of loneliness and craving as a post effect was more lethal than a bullet can be. I knew I wanted to finish our relationship, for uncertainty was the last thing I wanted in my life that time. Heart deceives and it was so undermined how easily it can fall in love. But love, did it exist or it was merely a sense of compromise. I had to question myself, if love was a settlement? Was I bargaining or were my feelings strong enough to let me take the leap. That I could no longer contain myself, that it was not worth to cause or receive any pain. I could not give it a try for I knew that if it fails me. I could no longer pretend to project any sanity outside, which I had been negotiating in the turmoil that I was fighting inside. I had no sufficing answers, but there was one thing for sure, I could not avoid his face and his thought from creeping into my head and heart. Though I wanted to let it go and not to occur to me. My own soul was rebelling against me, telling me that I was being unreasonable but I didn't know how to convince it. I had my soul to myself. He was captivating it and I hated the way he did it. The adeptness of his actions were making me even distant to myself and indulging him in me. I need to have myself to me. I hated that I had to surrender; I knew I would surrender then or later for it was getting beyond a point, which was out of my control.

Reasonable? No? That is the thing to hate the most about love. You're broken, you're shattered, you can't stop loving, and you can't push yourself away. You've to love them, it's a commitment, and it's a duty. Loving him was a part of my routine, missing him was not. I knew I was fighting something in which only defeat was subjected on me and my reluctance was only for namesake. I knew I had already lost. I had already handed him my crown.

Somehow, I gathered courage and picked his call, 'Hi, where were you?' he shouted as if nothing had happened. His voice had both tint of concern and anger.

'I... sorry... I didn't see your call.' I said trying to hide my confusion.

'I want to meet you,' he said.

'When? What happened?' I couldn't make any sense what was he up to. The last time we met it almost seemed he hated me, but he seemed to have forgotten that.

'When and where?' I didn't have enough courage to argue with him, for I wanted to see him so much deep down and didn't care about why he wanted to see me.

'At my home, I want you to accompany me and someone to my place.' His tone was so assertive, I couldn't even ask him whom I was supposed to meet.

'Okay, I'll be there in half an hour.'

'No, I will come to pick you up from the office, just wait for me.' His voice seemed more like an order.

'Okay.'

He was crazy, or at least he drove me crazy. It was impossible to rationalise anything for me. I wished that I knew what was going on in his mind. I was sitting at my desk while, I heard a symphony that was coming from the music room. I was confused who could be playing the piano at this hour. The music room was supposed to be closed. I decided to go and have a look that who it was. The door opened made a screeching sound as it opened and the music instantly ceased. I went inside with slow footsteps. A man in black hat was sitting; he looked towards the door as I moved in. He was old and must be about in his sixties, 'Can I come in?'

'As far I see, you're already inside.' He gestured his hands to take a seat.

'Am I disturbing, should I leave?' I politely asked.

'You must leave only if you are disturbed, for certainly you're not disturbing me.' He patiently said.

'Very well then, I think I should stay.'

I smiled and closed the door behind me. 'Why did you stop, kindly continue?' I insisted him to play.

'Do you know how to play piano?'

'Other than having touched the chords once or twice,' I frowned my brows.

'Okay I will play something for you.'

His hands tenderly went searching the board and his eyes closed. He pressed the board. The music room was sound proof meant no harmony was leaving from here and no disturbance was entering.

Calm, even more serene, the way a placid lake rested in its own boundaries, the symphony was roaming around reverberating from the walls of the room. Sometimes passing by my ears and leaving me numb. I heard the piano more closely to me. It absorbed the silence of room and I heard the mystifying essence of its creation. Hearty and real. Its vibrancy was playing notes on the highest emotional level, and stirring the quiet exterior that I was projecting. I let it hold me, and have all my attention. I could sense a feeling of divinity, a peace that I was alive. While he had not played the note for more than five minutes, I could read the entire silence that was secluded by the symphony travelling in the room. The void when I was devoid of the harmony, and when I was touched by its soft presence, like a feather.

I found myself in a dark forest sitting at the edge of a quiet lake, where the ripples were moving like the music in room. It was night, and there was a swan floating in the pond, giving rise to a new ripple with each new note. I heard the quietness of lake, disturbed by the paddling of the swan that floated silently on the surface, as nothing was going on beneath the layers of water. And then, there was another swan that joined it, floating in symphony, until the water started agitating against their united efforts. The swans paddled even more, and I could see their struggle now. It disturbed me to see the ripples shake violently. I wished to stop its turbulence and let the lake retain its placidity.

One, two, three and the agitation in water went on. I stood from my place to reach up to him. My eyes opened. My hands rested on his',

'Stop' I whispered.

His hands stopped on the board and without looking at me he took out a handkerchief from his pocket. I took it from him and left from there in silence.

'To live in certainty, you've to deal with uncertainty first.' he whispered.

I turned around, breaking from the spell. My eyes were filled with tears, brimming from the corner;

'Thank You'

I said and wiped off the tears with the handkerchief he had given me. I returned it to him and left. I waited for Gautam sitting in the lobby. These were the longest fifteen minutes of my life. I could still feel his compilation floating in the air even more than when I was inside. I wished I could ask him to play it again for me, but the way he stirred me with the pinnacle of innocence in his music, I knew I had fallen in love with Gautam even more. There was just an absence of five minutes. Each and every second that passed, I could sense it making me more certain of my love for him, and in front of his love I didn't matter. All that mattered was him. I went to the bathroom and looked in the mirror at least ten times. And then, there was a call on my phone.

I could hear my own heartbeats with thuds. I could finally sense myself breaking from the image I was absorbed in.

'Hello.' It was him.

'I'm coming,' I said and disconnected the call.

I went outside, to see him waiting. He was in a white shirt and blue jeans. His feet were in a Kolhapur. I could see his eyes gleaming, as he rested his back, on the door of car with hands crossed across his chest. His hair was unkempt. As I walked closer to him, my heartbeat increased. He stood straight, his hands unfolded by then. He started walking towards me. As we reached to each other, there was a silence for a while.

'I am sorry,' he said with a heavy heart and held me.

I hid in his arms, sobbing. He caressed my hair. He slowly parted from me, and pressed a kiss on my forehead.

'I want you to meet someone Avisha' and he walked with me to the car.

He opened the door and I saw Mr. Sharma there. His eyes made me recognise instantly that it was him. So, I greeted him. He must be in his late fifties. He wore a metallic black frame, with slight beard. His eyes were gleaming, similar to Gautam's and there was a glaze on his face. That same glaze that Mrs. Sharma had. He had a lean structure and must be five feet ten inches.

I was overwhelmed to speak anything. I turned my face to Gautam, and covered my face with hands. Again, he took me in his arms, while I sobbed in his shirt. But this time he was wiping the tears of joy.

He took me to the seat, and opened the gate. With tender hands, he made me sit. I looked at him, satisfied, and happy with tears. He nodded his head in approval and closed his eyes in assertion, assuring me. As he came to the driver seat, while he got in, I held his palms, speaking my happiness though my eyes. We headed for his home.

'I tried calling you so many times. Where were you?' he said

'I had left for home, and thought of leaving the job.'

He gave me a shocked look, and smiled. His head nodded again, this time in disappointment, and he rotated the key to start the engine.

NUMBNESS

I smiled at the thought of it, how surprised I was to have him in my life again, replaced by any other feeling. I knew that was the best gift God had given me after testing me thoroughly.

I was resolutely submerged in the feeling of peace. Gautam drove the car, at times saying a word or two to me. I didn't say anything but just nodded my head. It was a chilly weather, I looked outside and smelled the dew falling. And at times I turned to see the most beautiful person on earth next to me. I felt in peace till my innermost nerve was sure that life couldn't be more beautiful than being with person you love.

So calm, so serene, I drooled at the vivacious moment and thought if I could tie this to my soul forever. We passed several milestones. With every moment, I thought I would break, but I never did. I was just at the verge of it, but somehow, I always held on. I couldn't have though, if Gautam wasn't around.

I heard the tyres screech, and realised we had reached. Gautam asked us to get down. So, I got down and assisted Mr. Sharma in descending.

Mr. Sharma and I waited, while he continued towards the parking. I could sense the nervousness in Mr. Sharma's body. He was twitching and licking his lips every moment, so I went ahead to comfort him.

'It's going to be okay. Just relax.'

He looked at me and with an inquisitive eye. I held his arms and slightly pressed them. I settled his muffler, and he took out his cap and moved his hands in his salt and pepper hair.

'Does she still look beautiful?' he asked and looked at me with his lips pressed. A lot of his qualities matched with Gautam. His smile and gestures reminded me how when Gautam was nervous, he would often act in the similar way.

Settling his cap again, he bowed closer to me and asked again, 'Does she?' his eyes swaying between my left and right eye.

'She certainly is the most beautiful lady I have ever seen. You're lucky.' I held his arms. He raised his head in pride and delight, while Gautam came back.

'What are both of you talking?' he threw his keys in the air, and asked.

'Oh, nothing just something against you,' I said.

'I know a poor creature as me, with no one to love,' and he laughed a hearty laugh. He held Mr. Sharma's wrist and asked him to come along with him. I walked closely holding his other hand. His hands were shivering out of nervousness or cold, it was difficult to tell for sure.

We reached the door and Gautam pressed the button of bell. I saw Shreya running to open the door from the window. She quickly unbolted the door from inside.

She hugged Gautam and said, 'Back so soon. We missed you' and came ahead. I hugged and kissed her on the cheek. At first she ignored Mr. Sharma deducing her glances away. Then she shook hands with Mr. Sharma and said, 'I'm sorry I don't recognise him.' she stared at him for a while, then swayed his eyes between me and Gautam in confusion. Gautam moved his head to a side and pressed his lips.

I sensed the hands of Mr. Sharma was frosting and sweating by now. His grip was tightening. 'Is he...?' and Shreya eyes widened in surprise. I surely knew she was far more than shocked and didn't know how to express herself, so she ran inside to call Mrs. Sharma.

We entered the room, and the blower was on there. There was a sense of ease and I could feel the goose bumps on my face after feeling the sudden warm and cosy smell of home.

Mr. Sharma settled in the wooden chair kept by the table. His hands were joined, and looked like he was praying. There was an abrupt smell all of a sudden. It was the same smell of elegance that came out of the room of

Mrs. Sharma as the door of the room opened.

A lady in an off-white sari came out. With every step she took forward it seemed Mr. Sharma's heart pumped even loudly. His head was low and eyes looked high, in the eyes of Mrs. Sharma. Gautam went ahead and hugged her. He asked me to come along with him, to leave both of them alone.

As I got up to leave, she gestured me to sit. 'Whatever you've to say, please say in front of everyone.' Mr. Sharma's head was bowed low. He could not raise his head to meet her eyes, or to manage a word out of his mouth.

'Ma', Gautam tried to say something but she raised one hand gesturing him to stop talking.

'I do not have the strength to repeat it.' He said looking at Gautam.

'Then please leave,' Mrs. Sharma said without a tint of emotion in her voice.

'Don't say like this. I've waited too long for you. I can't anymore,' Mr. Sharma said in his crisp shaky voice.

'It doesn't matter.'

'It does Dimple.'

That was the first time I heard Mrs. Sharma's name.

'It doesn't anymore.'

'You want me to go. Can't you give me one chance to say what I have to?'

'I can't,' Mrs. Sharma said coldly.

Mr. Sharma put his hands on the table, supporting him to stand. The whole room was in a pour of heaviness.

'I deserve it,' he whispered.

'Wait,' Mrs. Sharma said.

'You married another woman. You left your family all alone behind. What are you expecting here?' she whispered with a confused expression on her face.

Mr. Sharma stared at her with an empty glance.

'I can't live without you.' he said.

His nose had turned red with cold. He smiled gently and hid me in his embrace. It was so cosy there. So warm, that all my sense of unease and panic left me immediately. I had the feelings of meditation.

'You know I thought...' before I could say anything further I saw Shreya.

In a moment remaining Shreya came outside. Her smile told that there was something going on in her mind.

'What is it?' Gautam asked her.

'What is this?' she pointed to us and hit Gautam with her elbow. Gautam held her and said,

'This is our family.'

We decided to go to a nearby cafe and have some coffee. So we started walking down the lane. The sun was dim, the air was chilling and there were long pine trees on the side of the road. It looked as if heaven were on earth, it had to be there.

Gautam smiled at Shreya and asked her, 'Do you want to ask something about father.' in an inquisitive tone.

'Well I am still shocked, and prefer not talking about it.' Shreya rolled her eyes and shrugged.

'I know, but he is not married to anyone else. He is still married to our mother. It's one of those imperishable love stories.' Gautam smiled at her.

'I don't know. Let's not talk about it now. I'll figure it out when I'm over the shock.'

'Okay.'

Gautam opened the door of cafe as we reached there. It was just a five minutes' walk from his home. All of us ordered cafe latte and picked it up to walk back our ways to home. As we had almost reached the entrance Mr. Sharma was standing outside.

Night was advancing and his face glowed in the lamp of the portico. He was holding a cup of tea and Mrs. Sharma was sitting on the chair kept over there. As we moved closer Mrs. Sharma's tears were visible.

'Is everything okay?' Gautam asked.

'Thanks a lot, son, for being there the way I could never be for our family.' Mr. Sharma said.

'I know you had your reasons, as long your intentions were not bad I understand. It may sound bizarre but somewhere I am proud of you, I don't know why. We had each other to take care of, and being taken care by. But, you were all alone there, keeping this spark alive. Though, I wish I never make this mistake in my life, and cost a lifetime to prove my love.' Gautam put an arm around Mr. Sharma's shoulder.

Then Mrs. Sharma went inside to prepare food and asked Shreya to take care of Mr. Sharma. I asked Gautam to drop me back home. Shreya insisted me to stay, but I had to leave as there was a lot of office work I needed to wind up. I bade them Goodnight and Gautam would drop me home.

I talked to Mr. Sharma and Shreya while Gautam went to get the car.

'It was great meeting you. I loved your company, though couldn't entertain you enough,' I said to Mr. Sharma.

'I would have definitely loved more of you around.' He hugged me.

'You will have me more often, don't worry.'

I hugged Shreya and waved them as I got into the car.

'What were you saying?' Gautam asked me as I settled in the car.

'When?' I was surprised by his question.

'When Shreya came.'

I put a little effort recollecting what I had to say, and realising what it was I chose not to tell him.

'It doesn't matter,' I said.

We had left from his place by then, and the road was dark, other than, at few places where there were street lights.

'Tell me.' He insisted.

'I am sorry, but I can't seem to recollect it' I was too afraid to translate the thought in words actually.

'It's okay,' he said, and let out a sigh. The disappointed look was evident from his face.

'Okay, I will tell you but please don't be angry after that'.

'You've to trust me to tell it,' Gautam said, pulling back his cheeks.

'When you maintained that bridge between us that day, on a mental note I wanted to drift away from you. I knew that thought was temporary and I wasn't going to act on it, but it hurt me deeply that moment.'

'Why?'

Gautam's brows frowned and he gave me a look as if I had committed some crime.

'I felt too scattered and couldn't seem to pull this thought of us being together anymore. It seemed like you didn't need me anymore.'

I bowed my head low and whispered looking at my wrist watch.

'If someday, I am unable to express to you how I feel about you, will you leave me?'

Gautam's voice had the tint of agony.

'That is not what I meant.'

I looked at him, trying to speak in my defence to escape the damage I had already done.

'Avisha, before this thought even occurred to you, why didn't you instead plan on killing me.' Gautam gazed at the road.

'Don't take it otherwise.' I held his shoulder and tried to speak what was on my mind.

'I am not talking anything otherwise.' It seemed as if he was pondering over something else.

'I was hurt, and couldn't figure out what was going on in your mind or what you wanted at that time. I thought, you mistook me and wanted to leave me there. I know I should have waited before preconceiving my notions, but it was a weak moment for me, as it was for you, and my head was eclipsed by the thought of losing your love. I wish, I could tell you how dearly, I love you, and how I can't imagine anything else other than you.'

'So, you figured out I wanted to leave you in anguish, and devastated all alone, without any trace of concern for our love? How deep you think I loved you? Is this... all these that you've understood me? Does it prove how strong our love is? If someday I become weak, instead of holding me, protecting me, you will choose to leave me.'

Gautam had tears, and I was ashamed that how did I end up hurting him every time, with my stupid assumptions.

'No, I didn't figure out anything.' I was panicking, I knew it was getting down the lane, that I hated it too.

'What should I understand Avisha, the only person I loved in my life had decided to leave me as I couldn't set my mind straight in a broken moment.'

His eyes had tears, and it killed me to see him going through all of this. That, which actually never existed and had nothing real. It was all my imagination that let that thought creep in, and now that was becoming his imagination making him comprehend the same.

'I am sorry, but you pushed me away...' I ventured saying something but he interrupted me.

'So you too pushed me away. Didn't you know what circumstance I was going through? You didn't know anything right?' He looked outside the window.

'Was my motto really to leave you and go?'

'I am sorry. I love you.'

'Let it be.' He whispered shaking his head.

'Let what be?'

'Let's separate,' he said with a voice so heavy, that I realised whatever he said came from his heart. I knew he meant it. It was too real to see our love fail. I choked, and couldn't believe my ears. How could a small thought in my head reach up to that conclusion?

'What are you saying?'

I couldn't look at him, and wiped my tears from my handkerchief rustling the words.

'What you've heard?'

'I'll die.'

Whatever I wanted to say, it seemed to have sublimed from my thoughts. Like I couldn't concentrate on anything. My power to rationalise had diminished, and I couldn't speak sitting beside him. He had made up his mind. I loved him, and living without him was not possible for the rest of my life. I felt thrown in the midst of the road we drove on, and Gautam walking away from me. Not reaching me, not even trying to. Everything came across surreal.

'So will I, but, I presume this is only to avoid the greater damage that might be caused in future.'

'I love you. I am sorry for thinking like that.'

'Your home has come, please get down I have more work to take care of.'

'Gautam...'

'I'll see you in the office, as we saw each other before.'

And in a moment, he was gone. I was left there all alone. I was left behind waiting for him, sitting on the stairs of my flat, waiting for his call. There was no sign of him returning, and with every passing moment, I felt more devoid of life. He was gone. Was he gone forever? Was it my mistake?

'Please come back.' I kept repeating in a low mumble. All alone, I didn't know what to do. I looked at the lane, and my eyes searched for traces of him. But, he was gone and it was for real. Howsoever I denied it he was missing from the present. There was no more of him. It was impossible for me to accept that he was gone.

I was sitting there with no feeling whatsoever, I couldn't relate to reality that everything between us was over. I got up from the stairs and went to sit on a bench near the parking. If he changed his mind and would come to see me, I could tell him how much I loved him. How I could not accept that anything between us could ever be over. How everything was just a stupid thought.

I knew he wouldn't forgive me. He will never take me back. He will never accept my weaknesses, for I was too weak. Too weak to handle him the right way. Too weak to protect him, when I was secluded from him.

My presence was entirely so shaken, that even if he came around, it was going to take moments, before I could realise it was him. The vent created was so dense that no fog of our emotion and love perforate either side. Was I so wrong, that anything I did was never right? I hated myself for never being able to express myself in the right way. For always pushing away the people I loved the most. Anyone, I loved dearly, drew this notion I don't know from where, that I didn't care about them. Why it happened? Why always? And if it had to be like that, why I ever got attached to him? Why did I ever fell in love? Why falling in love with him was not in my control? Why was I always blamed of abandoning my loved ones when they needed me the most? Maybe I was just a wrong person. Maybe I was one rotten soul. A soul that could never set things clear and straight. The more I tried to clear myself in the eyes of someone, the more it made me loose myself. And, bizarrely I always ended up with the blame on my head. The blame, which I duly accepted without rebelling against. The blame which was all on me. Always. Was I so selfish that I couldn't ever be forgiven; every small mistake of mine had huge consequences, that I was convinced that no one could ever be more wrong than I am? I sat there thinking how; I could never express myself in the correct manner. How I needed Gautam to just know how I loved him. How I wanted to be with him in silence and know that it was just him in my heart and I couldn't bear his distance. I was ashamed at myself. Ashamed because I hurt him, because of my inability to frame myself correctly. Ashamed that life was snatching him away from me, as I couldn't preserve him. I had to learn my responsibilities for what I did and said. I cried silently, sitting in the corner of my room, never demanding what I needed. Always accepting that maybe it was not in my share. Just letting it go by, but always waiting for it to return. Never going to fetch it. Never fighting to get it. What was mine will be mine, what wasn't will never be. And the dreadful part was what wasn't mine, was the one I loved the most. What wasn't mine was the person I loved the most. I loved him. Couldn't he see that? Couldn't he see what he was doing to me?

One hour passed he didn't return. Two hours passed he didn't return. And before I could realise, the night was already dense, I couldn't accept that he was not there with me. Was it real? God only knew. As the night turned pages of its book someone patted on my back. I turned back delighted, that he was finally there.

'Miss it's getting dark, you must return to your flat. It's going to rain.'

It was the night watchman. I stood up in despair and left for my flat. For one last time, I turned around to look at the gate. The rain started pouring, and I was all alone drenched in the rain that he loved. The rained I hated. But I didn't run to save myself from getting wet. I knew Gautam, wouldn't have, if it rained. For the first time in my life, I loved rain. *Sometimes we are accustomed to the habits of our dear ones, without them knowing.*

FOREVER

I entered the office with a numb heart. I was clueless how would I face him. I searched for him from the corner of my eyes and wore specs because they were swollen. I was feeling weak since the moment I entered the gate. My steps were not in sync with the brain. Each step provoked me to turn around and return. I didn't know how to pursue my eyes to lie. How would I confront him, and deny the love that reached his heart through and through? As I walked, everyone stared at me. It felt as they all knew what I did. They all knew I betrayed Gautam. Walking briskly, I reached my desk. Gautam didn't see me. I took a sigh of relief, as I sat on chair. I was determined I would not leave my seat for a moment. Coming from the entrance to my desk, was the toughest time in office.

I heard Kuber talking to someone and coming to me. He put a hand on my shoulder,

'Avisha, Gautam has withdrawn from the trip to Assam, so you'll be leading it now' he looked at me curiously, 'Are you okay, you don't look very well?'

'Oh, oh...yeah, yeah I am fine' I said trying to conceal my heart, which was trying to pump out of my eyes. Ignoring his statement, I asked him

'Why isn't Gautam going?'

'Um...' he took a deep breath, 'he is in the hospital.'

'What?' I felt the floor slipping beneath my foot.

'...uh...Where is he? Is he okay?'

In anticipation I grabbed my bag and got up to leave. Kuber scratched his head, perplexed if he should accompany me. But before he could decide anything, I had already left. There was a bunch of people standing in front the lift, so I took the stairs.

'What have I done? My cruelty has turned this obnoxious. If he recovers this time, I will leave everything and be with him. I don't need anything other than him.' I ran down the stairs. As I was exiting the office gate, I had an encounter with Jessica.

'Hey, hey, hey, where are you going in such a hurry.'

She stopped me holding my arm.

'I am going to see Gautam.' I tried getting rid of her grip and escaping.

'Whoa, wait, I will come to drop you.' and she joined me. She had a white scooter. I wore the helmet and sat on the back seat. We rode with lightning speed.

'I am going to tell him everything today. How I love him? How nothing else matters?'

In five minutes we reached the hospital. These were the longest five minutes of my life. Jessica went to park the scooter. I jumped out and ran to the reception. After enquiring all the details, I guided my path to his room, by taking directions from nurses on my way. Room number 319. Third floor. I stood in front of Gautam's room. I was overwhelmed by the feeling of seeing him. I knocked on the door. The door opened slowly. My heart beat was loud. That consciousness was now returning to me. It was Shreya; her eyes were inquisitive, as asking how did I come to know of it?

'Is he okay' I said toning down my anxiousness.

'Oh yes, come on in.' she asked me to come in.

I entered the room, looking behind her transparent body. My eyes were keenly looking for Gautam. He was sitting there. Jiah was beside him. He looked fine, laughing and talking to her. I was taken aback. While I was thinking he must be dying, longing for me. He laughed and acted as nothing had happened. I was head to toe submerged in humiliation.

'Hi,' he said arrogantly, but I could sense that blush on his face.

'Hi, how are you? I came to know you were admitted in hospital and I couldn't resist myself from coming. I was passing from here so thought of visiting you'.

'Um, how do I look? I am great. I've come for a routine check-up. The doctor said I am a fighter.'

And he laughed. I could sense Jiah fuming, and so was I, at both of them.

'Well I came here with Jessica. We were just going to watch a movie, so I thought I must pay you a visit. I was worried about the Assam festival'

How could I let myself be taken for granted? Not after watching him feasting the relics of life with Jiah. I gave him just a casual visit. Not that I was dying to see him; come-on, what was I thinking?

'Oh, where is Jessica?' I could hear the sarcasm in his voice.

'Uh, she just went for parking.' I told him, I will be waiting there, I dialled her number.

'I am standing near the reception. I don't know the room number.' she said in anger. 'Oh I am just coming' and I cut the call.

'I have to go, it's getting late for the movie.' And I went to Gautam, and even on trying the hardest couldn't control my feelings. I was evident from my eyes,

'Take care' and his eyes had the same look, like they said, 'don't go'. I heard him, he didn't say anything. But when I was leaving, I saw him struggling for words;

'Uh...' he pressed his lips. I didn't say anything, waiting eagerly to hear him, 'Th... Thanks for coming,' he said. I could see tears coming in his eyes. So, I turned around, gave a devilish look to Jiah. Before leaving, I turned around unconsciously and said,

'It would have been better if you lead the Assam trip' and before hearing his response I ran out of the room.

Coming out, I hit my head. What the hell was wrong with me? When would I learn to control my words? Cursing myself I ran from there. But, somewhere within I was happy that Gautam was alright. Still, I was fuming at him. Why that devil had always got to be around him? If it was in my control, I would have fired her.

In low spirits I descended the stairs. Jessica was sitting near the reception, reading the newspaper. I hit on her head from behind. She turned around in surprise.

'Where were you? Now, tell me what's all this about? Is he fine?'

Her hands were folded across her back. She looked inquisitively at me. I felt like dancing, I gestured her to come closer.

She moved her ear near me, 'I'm crazy in love with him.'

'Will you cut the drama, and just tell me?' her brows frowned.

'He's mad. I am just happy that he is fine. Kuber told me he is admitted into the hospital but he is here just for routine check-up' and I made the crying face of a baby. I put my arms around her shoulder, and moved towards the parking lot.

'I don't know what's all this going around, but he's okay. For now that is sufficient.'

I took Jessica by hands and swayed. She started laughing. There was mixed feelings on her face of surprise and confusion at my stupid reaction. She saw I acted in the weirdest manner today. In a way that was totally unlike me. While I should have acted in the most devastated manner, I acted as if nothing had happened. Maybe it was because I was sure of the feelings Gautam had for me. More that wanting him to be with me, I knew I loved him.

Jessica was still laughing, 'What are you up to? Let's go and buy some coffee,' she said and let out her tongue.

The sky was gray, and it looked like it was going to rain. I asked her to start the scooter and leave from there. I had to push her, to get the bike. For she wanted to buy herself a coffee because she was an addict.

I sat on the back seat. She was singing loudly, and got up on the seat to shout. Everyone was turning their heads to see what a fool she was. She just didn't care. She was the usual crazy herself, and at times it felt I better kill her, for the way she embarrassed me in public. Jessica commented at every other boy in the way while I hit on her head from behind.

'Drive straight, crazy girl. You're going to get us is some deep trouble one day.' I shouted to make myself audible through the curtain of air.

'Oh, my dear, when I'm here, why do you fear?'

I couldn't help but laugh, at her stupid rhyme. This whole journey seemed like some movie. It was cold and raining. I shivered at the back seat, while she enjoyed the ride. 'Woo hoo' Jessica's craziness was getting contagious, like always. But, I somehow managed to escape it. I knew someone needed to have their sanity to handle the situation. She accelerated the bike. We went on the river highway. She kept singing all the way. We had to cover the highway, for our next edition. So, we took a halt there.

When small drops of rain hit me, I trembled in cold. The weather was so chilly, that my fingers started to turn numb and purple. I took out the gloves from my bag and wore them. While, Jessica was just singing in a plain top. I gave her the spare sweater I had, and had to force her to wear it. Rain now had started giving me an utterly divulged sensation. It was totally new to me. It was crisp. Jessica was singing all the songs crossing her mind. I left her to do her what she was up to and went ahead to sit at the hill top. Hanging my legs down the valley. Though, as I sat there and looked deep in the valley my stomach churned and it felt my feet existed no longer. I rested my hands firmly behind on the rock after pulling the neck of sweater above. I was released of any feeling of guilt, any feeling of betraying him. I knew it was his choice, and love is not about possessing someone, as he had said. It's about loving someone, despite their choices. And I chose to love him, in all sanity, in all my senses. Now it didn't matter how it ended. I knew for long he was with me, and when he wasn't around now, he still sat beside me. I slapped the air, right at the height of his face.

'Crazy Man.' I sniggered.

The gray sky raised its curtain, allowing all the rain drops to kiss me. A tiny rain drops fell on my lips. I could feel it was frosting and I was sure about falling down with fever. Jessica was clicking pictures like a child, and I was enthralled by the feeling how connected she was to herself. I felt bewitched in the moment, at the beauty of the valley. If I jumped in the valley and died now, I knew it would be the most peaceful death for me. I was at the pinnacle of salvation. Crazy, crazy me. The scarf was floating in the air, slightly wet with the drizzle. I had goose bumps. I felt absolute in me, more than I ever had. I opened my arms, spreading it like wings, embracing all the air, with my eyes closed. That is when she started the bike on the river bridge, calling me.

So consummated, so endless, so calm, where was this feeling hiding till now? Why I never felt this before? We reached office two hours later. I was an entirely a different person then. Jessica stopped the bike on the gate. I hopped to the building. I greeted everyone, I saw on my way. The happiness was brimming from my face. I could read the surprise on their faces. That girl who always avoided people, she was greeting them on her own. I chirped, and felt on top of the world. I turned to see Nahel coming; he looked like 'Hercules' to me. Everything looked like a movie. He was still smiling. I blew him a flying kiss, he grabbed it. We laughed at it.

As I entered the office I was blushing. I went to Kuber's seat and gave him a gaping smile. He smiled back at me.

'So, when do we have to go for Assam' I asked him.

'Um...' and he laughed, putting his hands on the desk. I gave him a strange look.

'Gautam called just now. He is going. So, sorry you won't be leading the team.'

He smiled in embarrassment. I put my hands on his arms. He looked at my hands shocked at my reaction. I was the restrained one, who always maintained a hell lot of distance. Then in surprise he turned to me, 'Oh, the pleasure is mine' I said and laughed loudly. Gautam, yet another surprise; he was always taking me with surprises. The joy was evident from my face. I went from there. As soon I had left there was a call on my phone.

'Gautam', it read and I received the call.

My heart fluttered as I heard his voice.

'Hello' it was Gautam.

'I have to see you now' he said.

Without a pause I said, 'Where?'

'Near the coffee shop, on the outskirts of the city.'

'Be there in half an hour' and I disconnected the call.

I ran to check how I looked. But, it didn't matter what impression I had today. His love had made me enough beautiful, for my entire life. I clutched my bag and ran out of office. I hired a taxi and rushed to the coffee shop. It took me fifteen minutes to reach there. Gautam was already standing there.

My heart pounded. I felt the broken pieces connecting between us. I gave the fare, and asked the driver to keep the change. I stood at a distance looking at Gautam. He looked at me. We looked at each other. It was raining. He was fully drenched in rain. I was perfectly soaked in rain. I could hear a loud music out of nowhere. His eyes sparkled. My eyes gleamed. I smiled at him. He smiled back at me.

I ran to him. He didn't move. I hugged him, making him loose his balance. He was surprised. He put his arms across me tenderly. I cried.

He kissed on my forehead. I held him, jumping to reach the height of his ear. He smiled at me, and pulled me in his embrace.

'We don't get tired of fighting, do we? How do we find a reason to do it? I must say, it's an art. Fighting and loving, both at extremes, it's an art' he smiled.

'I love you,' I said.

Every time I said it, the grin on his face widened.

'Okay fine.' he shrugged and laughed.

His laugh stirred the chords of my heart, for I knew all the distances and dispersions were going. He felt it too, what I felt at the valley. The entire world seemed to disappear in front of my eyes. It was just him. It was just me. He bent on his knees, and looked in my eyes.

'Marry me Avisha?' he grinned. It seemed he already knew my reply. As he said it, he was embarrassed for displaying his love in this way, which was beyond his nature. Drenched in the raindrops, I put my head on his knees crying.

'You know it.'

'I love you.'

'Love never dies, it just changes forms. It just grows and finds new ways to express itself. I will never leave your side, and you'll never leave mine,' he said and he kissed my cheeks and hugged me. Tying my hands behind my waist he slid a ring in my finger. I held him while the rain did its job.